A
PRIVATE
LIFE

by Cynthia Propper Seton

A PRIVATE LIFE

A GLORIOUS THIRD

A FINE ROMANCE

THE HALF-SISTERS

THE SEA CHANGE OF ANGELA LEWES

THE MOTHER OF THE GRADUATE

A SPECIAL AND CURIOUS BLESSING

I THINK ROME IS BURNING

A PRIVATE LIFE

a novel by

Cynthia Propper Seton

W · W · Norton & Company
New York · London

FIRST EDITION

Library of Congress Cataloging in Publication Data

Seton, Cynthia Propper.
   A private life.

   I. Title.
PS3569.E8P7   1982   813'.54   81–11335
ISBN 0–393–01515–7   AACR2

W. W. Norton & Company, Inc. 500 Fifth Avenue, New York, N.Y. 10110
W. W. Norton & Company Ltd. 37 Great Russell Street, London WC1B 3NU

1 2 3 4 5 6 7 8 9 0

For my Mother,
Charlotte Janssen Propper

A
PRIVATE
LIFE

One

Aᴄᴛᴇʀ a long run of raw weather, on the fifteenth of October the continent of Europe woke to a morning of warm and balmy sunshine. It was a Sunday and immediately all the inhabitants got into buses and came to Paris. Never could there have been so many peaceful people spilling over the parks and into the avenues, into the Louvre and out again, up to the top of the Pompidou, through the maze of brisk businesslike rooms whose walls were hung with high-colored, rage-filled Berlin paintings—Grosz, Kokoschka, Kollwitz, Beckmann—Germans indicting Germans, very gratifying. Through the rooms and out again there moved the flow of people speaking every language, even French, and particularly German. They bought a colossal number of postcards. There is an intestinal quality to the new architecture in Paris at Charles de Gaulle and here at the Pompidou inspired, perhaps, by illustrated plumbing manuals, but appropriately so since it is intended to ingest whole populations at a gulp. At the top of the Pompidou many of the glass panes of its immense glass wall were able to be opened; like windows. A tremendous breakthrough. One could lean on a sill and breathe the Indian summer air and see the whole of Paris flat, low, and wide, stretching out into the haze. The sight was grand in one way, and reductive in another. The cathedral of Notre Dame, for instance, was undistinguished. Paris is not New York and should be seen from the ground up.

There is a small park in the back of the cathedral with benches, flower beds, and dog droppings—"More and more French people are substituting dogs for children," it was noted in *Le Monde*—and outside its paling twenty-seven superbuses from all over Europe and every part of France lined the narrow streets, their doors open, their tapes piping out Country and Western, and disco. Inside the cathedral on this afternoon there was a mass, spoken in a finely controlled elegant French with sonorous responses, and more sonorous organ chords, echoing through the loudspeakers and into the vaults. Perhaps a third of the people were participating in the service, the others milling, or stalled in the side aisles. Whether inside or out of the cathedral, the Beaubourg, the Grand Palais, the Petit Palais, the Louvre, the Palais du Sport, the remarkable thing was the absence of frenzy. Millions of individuals, all unwitting, had found themselves pressed into gigantic hordes, Cecil B. De Mille armies, numbers without end, and they didn't seem to break under the stress of it. In this they certainly proved themselves unlike rats. At the end of the day when the buses filled up and took off, there was left, it is true, a gigantic quantity of litter. It was this terrific mess blanketing the paths and flower beds that became the preoccupation of a frazzled-looking American woman of twenty-six who was sitting on a bench in the cathedral's little park. She was taken with the anachronistic yearning to bring order out of chaos, instead of vice versa, to be the one chosen to clean it all up. A sign of panic.

M.-E. F. Foote was in transit. She was at this moment on a Paris park bench, stalled by the wildcat strike of French railroad workers, but finally freed, after nearly four years, from the ignominy of a lowly clerical job in which her competence was never rewarded, never aroused any interest whatsoever. This job was at *First*, the suddenly successful New York monthly magazine which combined an interest in feminism with money, but not with Fanny Foote, which is what she called herself in New York.

"You know what I'm doing here, mama! I'm boring from within, and I mean boring!" she said to her mother, with whom she was in collusion over the phone bill.

"I don't see what you can do but stick it out, sweetie," which is what her mother called her in Boston, an uneasy mother who would slip ten dollars into the next letter, or even twenty.

Fanny was the sort of young woman who was having trouble settling even on her own name. Three factors had kept her at *First*. There was the panache of the association—"Oh, I'm at *First*." There was the miserable employment picture. And there was the very act of making it in New York, of showing her father, toward whom all her major performances were directed.

The management at *First* was a whirl of warring cliques and Fanny referred to it as The Mire, and the managing editor—called Candace by all in that grand little democracy—The Quoguemire, from her summer place out on the island where she was thick with the right people in the arts. One day Fanny was summoned to take notes by Candace, who looked at her thoughtfully, which was not her custom, and said, "Foote? Foote? You aren't related to Carrie Foote by any chance?"

"Oh yes, oh yes I am," Fanny said. "She's my aunt."

"Your aunt? Fantastic! Listen, I've been leaning on this for *ages*. I really think there's a terrific story there, a sort of Stein and Toklas story. Tavernier and Foote! And I mean after all, they have a claim to being *the* authentic feminists—*prototypical*. And on top of everything else you've got a really viable homosexual model there. Your aunt! What a godsend! Fantastic!"

Fanny, shocked to death, didn't blink an eye. She said with an air of quiet authority, "Oh, I don't think she'd submit to . . . she'd feel it was an invasion of privacy, you know . . ." It was at *First* that Fanny had had a real chance to watch the exploitative nature of men turn up in women.

"I *know*. Don't think I haven't had my lines out. The thing is *we* couldn't even approach her, but her own niece . . . I don't suppose she'd be coming *here* by any chance?"

"Oh no, she . . ."

"I think you'd have to go over anyway, feel your way into the *place*. You've been there?"

"Not really since I was a child. I . . ." In fact not really ever.

"Well, then, that's it. Of course you'll *have* to go over. How good are you with a camera?"

"Actually, I . . ."

"Anybody can take pictures. Listen, do you think you can handle it? *I* think you can handle it. I *know* you can," said Candace very sincerely. She must all at once have espied that fine competence in Fanny. "After all," she said reasonably if not accurately, "you're a Yale English major . . ."

"Radcliffe. But you know, Candace, I . . ."

"And you've been crying for attention. Okay. Here's your chance. Five thousand words, $500, plus expenses. Now the thing is it's got to be *intimate*, it's got to be *revelatory*—the *relationship* between the two—maybe *explosive*." To give Candace her due, for editors, for feminist editors in particular, old lesbians had become collectors' items. "And you know, places like that are always seething with intrigue, passions, affairs. You have to burrow in there . . ."

And so her mother had been right, and there might have been no change in her luck if Fanny Foote hadn't had the toehold.

She was tentatively Fanny Foote. She had been born Margaret-Eleanor Frances Foote, named for two grandmothers and called Megan. She had grown up in Boston and gone through college there. When she graduated she changed her name and went to New York to seek her fortune, sailed off high-hearted, free as the wind, and been more or less depressed ever since. She was not seriously clinically depressed but unpleasantly grounded, in part by her low wages, but also by the failure of freedom to bring extravagant returns, or even point the way. "I have asked myself, Miss Foote, whether the present generation of youth can be as shallow as it seems. I reject this on the score of probabilities," her right-wing professor of political science had confided in the middle of a seminar one day. She had bridled. She was outraged. She reported him to all her friends.

From time to time Fanny said to Missy, the woman with whom she now lived in partial squalor on 114th Street, "You know what I am? Shallow. I mean *really* shallow. I mean I have no substance at all. I'm just one tremendous act! One tremendous flop!"

Missy was in graduate school in anthropology, and said with professional calm, "In a narcissistic culture to be shallow is, actually, to adapt successfully."

"At home," said Fanny, "in the Museum of Fine Arts, there's that huge Tahitian Gauguin that covers the wall of a whole room, the one with the questions 'D'où venons-nous? Que sommes-nous? Où allons-nous?'—'Where do we come from? What are we? Where are we going?' Well, when I was really little I was embarrassed by the naked girls, but when I was about eleven or twelve, suddenly I made out the French, and I got quite upset about those questions . . . and my aunt, it was my aunt Carrie who used to take me . . . my aunt said she herself had absolutely no patience with people who ask questions like that—whence and whither questions. She said they're the kind who go on journeys in search of the pure and the uncorrupted, and everybody else has to pay for the journeys, you can bet on it. She said that each of us has to make up his own life . . . and not cry about it."

In public Fanny and Missy were indignant feminists but privately they shared more than their jeans and T-shirts: they shared a dismay in what Fanny called "the tin ear of our spokespeople." They craved to hear something to make their hearts soar. And a more mundane concern, which Missy expressed, "They're turning the best men mean or gay, an inevitable aggressive-defensive posture."

Both women were what is now called sexually active and were always trying to make a "relationship" last, make the sex turn into love, and their accumulated failure produced frustration: an unexpected contradiction. They referred to this failure as The Travail, had brooded over it constantly, and the upshot was that about three months previous to Fanny's gifts being discovered at *First*, they made a mighty pact to enter upon a one-year period of extreme rigor and self-denial in the matter of sex, become born-again virgins. They would also do evening swim at the Y and up the yogurt. They already jogged.

They entered upon an era of clean living, and Fanny, whose nature was the more given to enthusiasm, went about proclaiming her conversion. "I don't miss it at all!" she assured her several women friends, provoking some admiration and even inquiries. But Fanny said this once too often, evidently, because one day she found herself suddenly deeply frightened by the solemn truth that indeed she did not miss it at all, that there was something the matter with her, and that looking back she had always been . . . disappointed. She resumed feeling depressed.

So life proceeded and then two things happened to Fanny in a row. The second was the interview with Candace. But having no clue that rescue was at hand at *First*, and determined not to remain forever steeped in The Mire, she used her lunch hour sometimes to follow up a lead to another job. For this purpose she tied up her hair, put on the single skirt she owned, the hose and platform pumps, and decorated with this and that, she went off to breach the Establishment, a Trojan Clothes Horse. On this particular occasion she was leaving a PR agency, where her success had been in the breech and not in a job, and she was waiting for the elevator when a man came along who looked just like Alan Bates in *Zorba the Greek* and he said to her, "Did you press the button?" She wracked her head for an answer. Nothing. He pressed the button. "You aren't the new person in Seminars at Corporate Encounters by any chance?" he then asked.

"Actually, I'm not," she said crushed. "I'm at *First*," she added desperately, playing her only trump.

"Christ, you work for Candace?" He wore a dark suit, a shirt and a tie, possibly Gucci shoes, and carried an attaché case with the initials TX—wrong to the last cachet. He then said, "They told me they'd gotten somebody new in Seminars who really had it together and I noticed you had it together so I added two and two and got my usual five. I wouldn't mind getting a handle on Candace."

By the end of the elevator ride he suggested lunch. By the end of the lunch he suggested the night at his place. Things really move in NYC.

"My God, Missy, I've *fallen*," Fanny said, opening her account of the meeting with TX. "We had the most monumental pile of *junk* food. I broke *numero due!* But listen, on *numero uno* I was fortitude itself. I said no. I didn't explain, but I said no, and do you know what he thought? He thought I was very mysterious! He was *fascinated . . .*"

And Fanny, in turn, was fascinated by TX. In a week she had doubled her number of skirts and was in debt, and her feet were permanently deformed.

What intrigued Fanny about TX was his unwracked nature. There were men like that at school—business, economics, science majors who strode clear-browed through the Yard and the Square while the others, her sort— abstracted, soul-probing, eyes inward—could wander into them and get knocked over.

"Listen," she said to the dubious Missy, "he's interesting anthropologically. You can think of me as doing field work for you. I mean he belongs to a very successful new hybrid culture. Like a Cargo Cult. A lot like a Cargo Cult. On the one hand he likes money, success, anything you can put into a computer, and on the other hand he's really into ecology, he's antinuke, and about women, well, he has a sort of . . . chilly but sincere egalitarian philosophy—that everybody regardless of gender is equally interested to get what he is after . . . and of course he has that unreconstructed way of taking the check."

Fanny was at least really eating. TX knew a glittery city, walked her right through to the place on Second Avenue where people were pleading to be let in and the bouncer said, "Okay, TX," and they were allowed to sit at the bar and sip spritzers and be grateful to wait two hours for their table. However, it was certainly a break from health food, and moreover TX, who was not doubt ridden, who was not struggling with despondency, was also a cheery change, and Fanny found that she was returning to her neo-virgin bed laughing herself to sleep.

"I just don't get what you actually *do*," she had said to him.

"Well, you could say I was a liaison man. I mean Corporate Encounters is a big outfit and it's into public service. We *call* it public service, which testifies to our creative imagination. Now, my division is Polling in Depth. Listen, baby, you wouldn't *believe* the kind of stuff some people want to know. So of course we have this terrific data-amassing department from which we learn that there are an estimated 700 million unfilled cavities in this country. You didn't know that, did you? Or take the ant. Do you sometimes wonder where the ant gets his *strength?* Well, this'll flatten you. The sly little bugger makes his own Vitamin C! That's why he has so few colds!"

She asked him what he really wanted out of life and he waffled, said he had a lot of ideas, confidence, that he meant to hang loose, and his short-term goal was the three-martini lunch.

She sighed and said, "You narcissists, you have everything going for you."

He said, "I'm not a real narcissist. A lot of it is circumstance."

For his part TX was charmed by his letting Fanny deflect him for a little while from his forward thrust on all fronts. He thought it testified to a warm authentic self (in him), and while he wasn't into the self-flagellation trip, he was not a man of inactive conscience. However, Fanny had turned up just at an awkward time when he was suffused by an exhilarating sense that his life was on the point of takeoff. So that when he, of the scanning eyes and swivel-pipe neck, thought of her from the point of view of utility, she had none. She could not even deliver on Candace. And actually physically, he thought she was too big, although he was always attracted to proud-looking women and they tended to run big. Still, she kept him bemused. For instance, she said she was a list keeper. She carried a notebook where she kept her lists up-to-date. She had a very long master list of the Finest People Who Ever Lived and almost all the names were crossed out. In fact at the moment there were only Keats, Marcus Aurelius, Chekhov, Peter Rodino, and Pavarotti. He found it astonishing.

"Oh well, there have always been list keepers—since Homer. You haven't run into them, that's all."

"I just don't understand the point. I'd *really like* to *know* if there's a point," he said kindly but seriously, "or whether it's just kinky."

"I have noticed for a number of years," Fanny said sternly, "that there's been a shortage of fine people." She looked to his eyes for corroboration but did not find it and went on, "Of course when we were children the world was full of heroes and heroines and stars, and they were all American, but I always remember a piece of information that startled me when I was in third grade. It was the grade when you learned about Fulton's Folly and McCormick's reaper, how we invented everything. But then Miss Murphy, the teacher, said although Thomas Edison gave us the electric light and the phonograph he was quite a nasty person. Well, I guess it was my first intellectual shock . . . that things weren't going to be *tidy* . . . that you could *do* good and not *be* good . . . and, more and more lately, that you could *be* good and not *do* good. Now if I kept a list of *that* group I think you could say it was kinky. But my list gives heart. It reminds you that people, all the way to the top, can be very fine, that it is not just a discredited romantic or sentimental idea."

TX wondered if there wasn't something in Fanny after all that could be put to use, and this thought made him look very attentive.

And by the time of the Candace interview, several days later, Fanny wondered if there was something in TX after all.

Two

FANNY and Missy were not interchangeable, and in their friendship Missy had the natural advantage. Principally this was because it was not in Missy's nature, or rather not in the nature of her knees, at the first sight of a crossroad, to buckle. Missy progressed. Turning points? She turned. Tips of icebergs? Over the top. Not Fanny. Uncertainties of a really useless nature (*pace* TX) kept her shuffling about in Square One. She was harried by whether it would have been better to live in London in 1815, when Keats might be passing on the street, or in 1860, when Darwin might, or in Cambridge or Oxford in 1905, in which case she would, ideally, have to be a male homosexual. She was not unmindful that by the time Keats was twenty-six he had been dead a year. These hovering and vague preoccupations with the texture she would like her life to have held her back from advancing into the future in New York. Missy did not approve of Fanny's drift. She assumed the responsibility for getting ahead and hoped that by precept and example Fanny would follow.

But not by leapfrogging.

Missy had already been put out over Fanny's easy seduction by this TX. She thought that if it weren't for their vow of renunciation, he would have been in and out of her system by now, another irony to ponder. And certainly Fanny was aware that her infatuation with TX was irksome to Missy, and the little friction it produced was even a little gratifying. But on the evening she headed home after her amazing interview with Candace, when fate, all unbeknownst, had swooped down and plucked her from tedious obscurity and assigned her Success, Travel, Romance (more or less what one waits for fate to do), Fanny was aware that by Missy's measure this award was unmerited, that Fanny didn't deserve it, and that it would disturb the equilibrium of their friendship. She intended, therefore, to tell her story quietly, to be tactful.

"You're not going to believe this. This is going to blow your *mind*," she said to Missy in a voice that intended to carry unworthiness. "Candace is sending me to *France*. I mean it's the most bizarre piece of luck because when I walked in there she didn't really know which one I *was*. But all of a sudden something clicked in that computer brain of hers and she asked me whether I was related to Carrie Foote. Well, it turns out she's had this thing about a story about Foote and Tavernier, but she says she's never been able to get them interested. And so when *I* turned out to be the niece, there was absolutely no winding her down."

"You told me that there was a family feud and that you hadn't seen your aunt since you were six or something," said Missy, in protest and in control of her enthusiasm over Fanny's good news.

"Twelve. I was twelve when she decamped with Mrs.

Tavernier. I don't think anybody's been on speaking terms *since*. I don't know what it was all *about*," said innocent Fanny.

"It's always about money or sex." Missy at least wasn't into innocence.

"I understood it was a question of *loyalty*. It was the first time my father was running for Congress, and he was counting on her, and varoom! she cut out! Oh, good grief, I was *desolate*. I really *loved* her, I wanted to grow up and be just like her, but . . . probably I'm the last person she'd care to see."

"Did you tell Candace that, about the feud?"

"Don't you know I've never been to *Europe?*" Fanny snapped. She was ready for a little more support. "Don't you know how I *crave* to go to Europe? Anyway you can't *tell* Candace anything."

Missy struggled to put down a querulous tone, and after a moment she said, softened, "I wonder why she is so anxious for another story on them."

About the Printing House, which was the name of the pension owned by Tavernier and Foote in the small city of Albi, some place or other in France, Fanny as well as Missy knew only what they read in the occasional literary article and occasional literary or musical references. It seemed that Tavernier and Foote were two so much admired women that people of renown—writers, musicians, scholars— periodically felt the need to live there for a while, settle into this pension of theirs, and get their work done. It wasn't a month ago that Missy had shown Fanny mention in the *Times* of Junie Waterman, who lived at the Printing House, and who had been over for the publication of a new book.

"I mean," said Missy, all quiet reason now, "that you can see that if a writer like Junie Waterman takes the trouble to hole up in a virtually inaccessible place like Albi, he really doesn't want to be tracked down and trotted out by any Candace. I mean it's understandable. If they wanted to be lionized, after all, there are plenty of places . . ."

"She's taking another tack . . . the lesbian element . . ." said Fanny, uneasy and wanting to confess, and she described Candace's enthusiasm for the homosexuality of her aunt and Mrs. Tavernier.

Missy, ruffled again, said sharply, "You never told me they were gay!"

"I couldn't have been more astounded! I'm absolutely *certain* my parents don't have the least suspicion."

"Well, then, where does that leave you, I mean morally?" said Missy, indignant.

"Well, I hope you don't think I would go over there and do something despicable to my own family, to the people I love!" said Fanny, also indignant. "My intention is to take advantage of *Candace*, and get over there and betray *her*, that's all. I don't call *that* despicable.

"And in fact," Fanny said after a moment, "this is going to test my character in a very visceral way, because in the first place I'm going to have to confront *reality*, namely my *father*." Fanny had the sort of father who was waiting for his overgrown daughter to pull up her socks and get on with it. His name is legion.

"I think, after all, I'll do that in the second place. My mother . . ." Fanny tried to remember what part her mother had taken in the feud.

Fanny called her mother and said, "Listen, mama, something really complicated has come up. What's the possibility of your flying down this weekend?"

"Are you all right?"

"Great!"

"Well, this weekend is out. I've got the most *immense* obligation. Nothing must distract me. Right out of the blue we've been chosen by the Neilsen Rating people to tell them what we watch on TV for one week, beginning Thursday," said her mother, the clown. She had been reading up on Separation Anxiety and the mother was to have a Low Profile. "We've got a *diary*. We've got instructions galore. I have to fill in Man of House, Marcus, 56, Woman of House, Elizabeth, 56 . . ."

"My God, mama, you hardly ever look at the thing!" Fanny was laughing.

"Don't be foolish. I've waited more than half a century for power and influence. And besides, they've sent us fifty cents. We've *taken* the *money!*"

"Well, bring the diary along and I'll *help* you."

"Oh you *can't*, Megan. We're on our *honor*. And there's a place for *Guest*, and you can make *Comments*, and actually, sweetie, I don't want them to think we lead a dreary uneventful life. I was thinking of 'Guest enters. Fierce struggle for control of channels ensues. Guest thrown out!' "

"Now listen, mama, what I have to talk about is Even More Important. It's about Carrie."

"Carrie?" Her mother's voice changed. She sounded truly surprised and Fanny decided to push her advantage on the phone. She delivered a carefully edited version of her interview with Candace. "I mean Candace sounded positively *reverent* about the kind of person Carrie was, and really felt that what she and Mrs. Tavernier had accomplished—the sort of Alternative Life-Style, not to mention the Ambiance—well, she really thinks the public has a Right to Know, that there's a sort of Moral Imperative about it," Fanny elaborated, mocking up the conversation unfairly. Even Candace didn't talk like that. She stopped herself in mid flight, not wanting to put her mother off, and an octave lower, she said, "It's a real break, mama. I get my regular salary, plus $500 and expenses. You know I've never been to Europe. And they've given me a *camera* . . ." She waited.

Her mother was quiet for a long moment and then said casually, "I think it's wonderful. It's an opportunity for you to get reacquainted with Carrie now that you're grown. She was always the finest member of the family."

Fanny was very surprised at her mother's calm reception of her news. She asked, "Do you really think she'll agree to see me?"

"I don't *know* but I think she'll adore the idea. She certainly loved you when you were little."

"Well, what about . . . dad?"

"Well, he won't adore it."

"Well, okay, I'm going to have to think things out a little."

Fanny thought about her father, the most admired of lawyers, the greatest civil libertarian, First Amendment Foote, for eight years a pillar of integrity in the halls of the United States Congress. People would always tell her she must be proud of such a famous father. Unnecessary. When he retired to return to his practice in '74 his name dropped like a stone from the columns of the *Globe*, she noticed.

Three

FANNY'S father, Marcus Foote, was said to have the luck
of the Irish without the trouble of being Irish, and the gifts
of the Jews without having their problems. For eight years
he had represented a congressional district in the greater
Boston area, where these two groups were in domicile, and
he had been so popular he twice ran for reelection unop-
posed. He had been born in that very district. His father
had been the principal of a junior high school and his
mother had taught music with a pitch pipe. They were people whose heroes began with Woodrow Wilson and Al
Smith, Justice Holmes and Justice Brandeis, and ended
with Eleanor and Franklin Roosevelt, although they themselves lived on. They believed in bringing the light of reason to the benighted, most of whom were beyond their
reach in the parochial school system. Marcus Foote grew
up with a lot of hoodlums from this system, and the hoodlums never forgot him. "It's a darlin', darlin' district!" was
his rallying cry in the basement of St. Polycarp. And on
the other hand he was still such a regular attendant at bar
mitzvahs that he had his own yarmulka. The Jews seemed

to believe that a fairy put him in the wrong cradle. He was short, stocky, and dark, like his mother, whose people came from southern France. As for the Blacks, they began to move in numbers into the district at the end of the sixties but they never did think Foote was Black.

Foote admitted he wasn't Irish, Jewish, or Black. He went further. At the height of the Vietnam crisis, when the students were in a real frenzy, he also became an honorary youth—this was a rather late development—and he marched and wept with them even though they weren't his constituents. To his constituents, untold numbers of whom did not at all admire the students, he took the part of interpreter. He would put down his notes and walk to the edge of the platform and tell a hall full of angry patriotic transit workers how in 1941, when he was a freshman commuting on the Lechmere trolley and the Nazis were winning the war in Europe—"And America was *letting* them, letting France fall, letting England . . . and of course you're at that rebellious age, you know. You're already fighting the old man about every blessed . . ."—well, one bleak afternoon the tension snapped in him, and he hopped off the Lechmere and onto the Beacon Street and went off to join the Communist Party!

"A hair's breadth! I was a *hair's breadth* from . . . I got out at Copley Square and there was the *Traveler* just hitting the streets, with a banner headline: HITLER–STALIN PACT!"

He was known for his candor, evidently a winning characteristic.

"He's always bragging about his sins," said his enemies.

"I do not brag about all of them," he said.

In the Foote household during the dismal years before Watergate there were a lot of youthful rebels: the father, the two older boys, Buddy and Tom, and Megan, who was peering from the edge of childhood at the odd dissolution of family order, which was making a shambles of what she had believed to be immutable laws of behavior. The mother really had her hands full for a while. In those days parents of the anguished nature of Elizabeth and Marcus Foote yielded the last remnants of homely certainty, of domestic authority, as they joined their children on the same fields of outrage and protest. The Cambodian incursion? Marcus Foote knew Bud's, Tom's, Megan's despair twice over. He'd *been* there. Hadn't he, when he was seventeen, nearly joined the Party? It was very hard for children to effect a separation from a father and mother of so much under-standing, and it looked for a while as though they'd need an extra ten or twenty years to do the job. Tom had taken seven years to get through college. And now Megan had become Fanny, was stalled trying to become Fanny, whoever that was.

Fanny had not been home in months for dermatological reasons. It was where her skin broke out. At the last moment on Saturday morning and out of the blue, she told herself, she took the Boston shuttle for a quick surprise visit with the intention of being back in New York before her skin had realized what had happened to it.

"Actually it is not going home at all," she argued to that unconscious self in charge of corporal punishment, much as Alice scolded her feet in the days before Freud. "Home! They *sold* home!" By which she meant that her parents had sold the old house, once the children were out, and had moved into an apartment at the bottom of Beacon Hill. Her father could, now that he was back at his old law firm, walk to work. The apartment was not without charm, a kind of fancy railroad flat on the top floor of a rundown town house which had been renovated but had managed to keep some of its original rundown quality. Through the kitchen window one could see a bit of the Charles, with, in fine weather, hundreds of white sails tacking around the Salt and Pepper Bridge. It was a grand sight, the only view in the house. Fortunately both parents had a consuming interest in food and were in a position to look out of this window a lot.

Marcus Foote was in fact in the kitchen when the doorbell rang. Annoyed, he washed the oil off his fingers and walked the length of the house to the door, not before the bell rang again. And there before him was his daughter, a great big American Juno, the beautiful color of health, of youth, even with her hair looking like a magpie's nest, even with the army shirt, the rucksack. He thought she could have stepped out of a recruiting poster for the air force (AMERICA NEEDS YOU!). And from the moment of her arrival he was exhausted in advance by her energy.

"Didn't we give you a key?" he asked, for greeting, but in a pleasant voice, not betraying the exhaustion-to-be.

"Daddy!" said Fanny, who was destined to be the one surprised on this surprise visit. "I'd expected it would be mama. Goodness, I haven't seen you in *ages.*"

With clogs on her feet Fanny was a tallish girl with a shortish father, and this extra height combined with her nervousness at being greeted by the wrong parent caused her to regress about ten years, to hug him extravagantly, and in general bubble over, patting him several times as though it were he who was flustered. "You look great!" she said, not seeing at all that he looked harried, and finally, the greeting near an end, she gave a sophisticated wriggle to her shoulders to fling off her backpack, and unfortunately it hit him on the cheek.

Now her father did not feel great to begin with, and he had to suppress this further evidence that he was under siege.

"You're just in time," he said, giving a small tug to the tip of his nose, his way of settling himself. "Come on into the kitchen. It's a good thing I put up four eggs, isn't it? I'm making up a little antipasto and I'm in the middle of the dressing."

"I didn't know you'd taken up cooking!"

"It was cooking or jogging. Now see if there's a can of Norwegian sardines, will you?" He returned to the dressing, to which he devoted his entire attention.

"Where's mama? Will she be home for lunch?"

"Turmeric? Smell it. What do you think?"

"Is mama all right?"

"Fighting form and off to see her mother," said Marcus, pleased to mislead his daughter with the facts of a murky matter. "Will's got two tickets to the game," he added. The Red Sox–Yankees game. There is a commitment to attend this game which supersedes all other commitments including filial, which, if you live in the Commonwealth, needs no justification.

Fanny immediately saw her large, intractable, querulous grandmother sitting stiff-backed in her room in a residence for the elderly run by the broad-minded Quakers God Bless Them. She was accustomed to wrap herself in quilts and looked like a giant tea cozy. Fanny had a somewhat guilty love for this grandmother, nearly ninety, who had been discovered to have, at a very early age, a lust for control and power which was destined to produce ulcers, migraine headaches, arthritis, and hypertension in others. The residence was about an hour north of Boston near the New Hampshire line.

"Oh, I'll call her! I'll rescue her," said Fanny, in fact off to rescue herself from a terrible ungainliness she felt when alone with her father. Would the day never come, she wondered, when she would behave before him with an easy, unaffected maturity? Probably not, so unreasonable are the conditions of this sort of mutual love.

"She's not there yet," said Fanny, back from the phone. "But grandma sounded terrific, really enthusiastic about mama's wasting her time. She said she'd send mama right back as soon as she put her foot in the door. I warned her she'd better give her her tea."

"Ah, there's a woman gets her pleasure from plans going awry if they're not her plans. Long trip up there and ping-pong back to Boston."

Marcus, meanwhile, had completed preparations for their lunch, the kitchen table quite elegant with wine glasses, and father and daughter set to it. They talked at odds. Finally, Fanny, who had wondered all this time how she could parry the question what brought her home, abruptly reversed track—an example of what in philosophy is called the Catastrophe Theory—and, a little piqued, asked, "Don't you want to know what brought me home?"

"I don't think I'm going to keep turmeric in my repertoire," said Marcus, a master parrier himself, who knew why his daughter had come home. He knew that the subject was his sister Caroline, a subject around which he and his wife had tripped cautiously until this very morning, when Elizabeth, without warning and wanting in all delicacy, said, "Listen Marcus, you've got to clean up this business about Carrie. That story about denying you the money for your campaign, I didn't believe it then, and I don't believe it now." They had been sitting over their breakfast coffee, each with his own section of the *Globe*, and she shot him like that, right between the eyes.

He was outraged. He had drawn himself up in dudgeon as anyone would who had constructed a story that went unquestioned for so many years that even he himself felt entitled to believe it. After several moments he said, his eyes very wide, his voice very deep, "I must say, Lizzie, I think it's *extraordinary* that you have been able in easy conscience, as it seems, to live with a man while harboring such a doubt for what is it? Fifteen years?"

"I wasn't harboring a doubt," she had said flatly.

Now Marcus said to his daughter in a mild, easy manner, having had several hours for reflection, "Mother told me they've asked you to get an interview with Carrie, that it might be the break you've been looking for."

"Well, daddy, I know that you and Carrie had an *awful* quarrel but it was such a long time ago, and you know, it's really *unlike* you to nurse a grudge, and I thought . . . I know it is *definitely self-serving*, but it is not only that—I thought I might even be an emissary . . ." Fanny threw her soul into this wandering sentence, in a passion to come out of the end of it still her father's girl.

"Quite right," he said briskly. "You ought to know her. An exceptional woman. And I may say now, notwithstanding painful provocation, you know, that I was in the wrong. I was definitely the one who was wrong. It was my first campaign, '66, and I was prickly about things . . . you know, *loyalty*. And of course there was the excitement, all the attention . . . I suppose it went to my head. Touch of hubris, I'm afraid . . . It was clear to me later, you know, when the damage was done, that I might seem to have been riding roughshod over, well, let's say, the *sensibilities* of

other people. Yes, really, Carrie was certainly entitled to
. . . anyway, I had been thinking about a rapprochement
and here you are, my blessed peacemaker." He smiled at
his dear girl, lifted his glass to her, a toast to the truth. To
say mea culpa is always at least to some extent disarming,
and indeed, exculpating. Not everybody did it well.

For Fanny this particular confession cleared the obstacles
to her project with a swoop. She was at first limp with love
from the charming candor of her father, and many minutes
passed before she could think where she was and what to
ask next.

"Well, now, did you know Mrs. Tavernier?"

Her father, his brow furrowed, poked uncertainly at his
stomach. "What do you suppose turmeric is? You don't
think it's what they put on their poison darts? Well now,
I've got to run. I'll tell you all about her when I get back."

Four

WHEN no young were visiting, the study was the room in which Marcus usually slept, a consequence of a cultural revolution that was effected during the move from the old house. The revolution was not, as might be thought, in the assignment of separate rooms, a mutual and amicable attempt to reduce the discomforts of insomnia on the one hand and low back pain on the other. But just as the Chinese students were sent "down to the countryside" to narrow the gap between mental and manual labor, so Marcus would have henceforth to make his own bed, and other novelties. Every morning, over more or less unstraightened linens, he pulled a large kilim he'd picked up in Ankara when he was on a junket. In a lumpy way the kilim lent an appearance of Oriental luxury to his study, giving it the look of the room in a seraglio where they went to improve the mind.

Lonely Fanny, after a desultory stroll through the shops on Charles Street, came back to poke through the apartment where there was no evidence of her immensely significant childhood. She ended up on the kilim, propped against the pillows, with a map of France, waiting for the return of one or the other parent. At last her father came back with a forlorn face from the Red Sox having lost, and although he was obviously anxious to review the events of this game, pitch by pitch, he was not without a sense of justice, and delivered himself over to his daughter's preoccupation.

"Well, first of all, daddy, she was an opera star, is that right?"

"Lutécie? Couldn't sing a note." In the event, this was not true.

"Oh? I thought she was a sort of prima donna at the Met or something. I thought . . ."

"Well, she had once been a prima donna of the opera world in *her way*, you see. She was just a girl when she married Tavernier, and he, at the time, was a great tenor, much older, twenty years, anyway. Actually, to speak literally, Lutécie had no talent for doing almost anything whatsoever. *Being*, she had *being*. That's what it was! She was one of those rare creatures with what Darwin might have called a *monstrous* capacity to fascinate men, *successful* men. She would have been a star of any world, Wall Street, Washington, or wherever, but as it happened, Tavernier scooped her up. And so she assumed the what-do-you-call-it, accoutrements of the great diva, principally in the collection of a series of lovers of the Greek Shipping Magnate variety. And of course that's why people naturally thought she must have had a great voice."

"Well, did you ever meet her?"

"That's it, you see. I got to know her quite well through Carrie. Carrie knew her, *befriended* her. In France, I think. Lutécie was French, she was born in Toulouse. In any case, at the time I got to know her poor Lutécie was in great emotional turmoil with a pile of personal troubles including a rather tricky lawsuit . . . and that's how I came in."

"And did *you* find her that . . . attractive?" Fanny knew her father to be a man whose admiration for women was uncomplicated, and she listened for some hint that Mrs. Tavernier's "monstrous capacity" was perhaps too polymorphous for his tastes.

"I'll tell you the truth, Megan," said her father, bending towards her in his most confiding manner. When he was telling the truth he was the soul of honesty. "She was certainly past forty when I met her and there was *still* nobody in her league. 'Age cannot wither her, nor custom stale her infinite variety!' Cleopatra! Hard for a girl to imagine, I expect . . . that much *magnetism* at a certain age." Cleopatra and Antony were Marcus's favorite lovers for their being thirty-nine and fifty-one respectively at the time of their fatal passion. He now heard the sounds of his wife's return and after a moment's pause, he added in a clear voice, "I always knew how to appreciate an older woman. Look at your mother!" Elizabeth was six weeks his senior.

Elizabeth now entered the study. She was a woman with the shape and color not unlike the queen of the same name—the perm, the corseting, good English skin—but with a clear-eyed manner that suggested she would have abdicated before she was thirty, bringing down the government.

"For heaven's *sake*, sweetie, why didn't you tell me you were coming?" she said. "I wouldn't have gone off, and they have shrimp on sale at the Star Market."

"I was certain you'd be home, mama. I thought you'd be glued to the tube."

"She only watches Barney Miller and Reginald Perrin.

They're going to get this whole diary with nothing in it but Barney Miller and Reginald Perrin. She won't put down what I watch."

"I won't put down trash. I *will* just wash up."

"Daddy says Lutécie Tavernier was quite a fascinating woman," said Fanny when her mother was settled in.

"Oh, I don't know!" Elizabeth said.

"I was only telling Megan that many men, my dear, as well as many *women*, found her charm . . . ineffable."

"I found it effable."

"Caroline, after all, followed her clear out of the country, dropped her own life on a dime, cut her moorings, abandoned *all* of us . . . positively apostolic, seemed to me . . ."

"Carrie *rescued* her. She was with absolutely no resources if you don't count her money and her looks."

"You put it that way, one of course *sees* . . ." said Marcus.

"What do you mean, 'rescued,' mama?"

"Oh, there was some man or other who wouldn't let her go, some very rich man . . ."

"One of those Greek shipping magnates," Marcus added.

"*I* think it was the Scottish earl," said Elizabeth with authority. Elizabeth was invested with authority.

"What your mother means is that just about this time Lutécie came into an inheritance—in fact the pension in Albi. Well, you see, the will was contested by some collateral relatives living in Toulouse, but of course we won, and so, rather quixotically, *I* always thought, they went off, the two of them, to run the thing."

"It is inconceivable that Lutécie could run so much as a bath," said Elizabeth. "It was Carrie who had the mind, the energy—who had the necessary generosity of spirit . . . to provide for other people's needs."

"You forget that Lutécie had an excellent taste for cooking, a sense of cuisine. To be fair," said Marcus.

"She liked good food. We all like good food."

"But you know," Fanny said, "I think it is curious—what I don't understand—is why Carrie would suddenly leave a profitable academic career to run a—well, actually what sounds like a *boarding* house—to rescue somebody I mean who is just after all only, well, a *friend* . . ."

"Yes, of course, that was it *exactly*," said her father. "I was really angry at the time that she would . . . throw away a *promising* academic future . . ."

"You're mad," said Elizabeth flatly.

"Now *why* do you talk like that, Lizzie?" Marcus said, benign voice, all reason, foolishly breaking his rule against asking a question whose answer he didn't want to hear.

"I can't under*stand* you, Marcus. That was the entire problem. She had *no* promising career, couldn't get her promotion, thought she would never earn tenure, because she was a *woman*. She was just matter-of-factly beneath consideration because she was a *woman*. Countless times she asked you about it, wondered whether you would be willing to consider taking it on as a civil-rights case . . ."

"My God, you *forget* I was making my first run for Congress! I was up to my eyeballs! Sixty-six. You forget there was no real women's movement yet. You talk with the perfect vision of hindsight!"

"*You* forget what a burning issue it was for her. Remember the night we had dinner at the Ritz? She brought Lutécie? Oh, she *adored* you, looked up to you with, I must say, *unaccountable* confidence, she . . ."

"Who?"

"Who? Carrie, for heaven's sake. She revered you, the older brother, everything you did, fell for it all, and what was she? Thirty-five, thirty-six? Lutécie was old enough to be her mother."

"Ha! You're crazy."

"Ach, why do I let you get my goat," said Elizabeth, suddenly, and to her daughter she said, "It was a sad time for Carrie. What I suspected was that she had fallen in love with . . . well, I believe it was a married man."

"Is that so?" said Marcus.

"She was filled with compunction! She was riven. I suppose you can hardly believe that people in living memory had consciences like that, Megan. Honor, integrity, self-control, the highest standards, *that* was Carrie. She had *character*, that's why she fled, *I* thought. Of course it doesn't account for your father's . . ."

"Could be a little rigid," said Marcus.

". . . *indignation*," said Elizabeth.

"Stuffy sometimes. Stuffy from a child," said Marcus passively. But as he now saw that his wife and daughter were looking to him for the explanation of his unwarranted behavior in 1966, he began to shift about, and explain in a tone that was somewhat agitated, "Listen, Lizzie, honestly, I can't *recall* why I should have reacted so extravagantly over the money. We'd come into a little inheritance, Megan, and I thought she'd pitch it in, you see, but . . . she took it with her." On those rare subjects upon which he felt he could not be candid, Marcus experienced sincere distress. "There isn't a man in Congress who doesn't believe that all members of his family are happy to sacrifice their own lives for his favorable wind," he added, so that his wife would not have to bother.

They discussed for a few minutes whether this was any longer true, and then Elizabeth turned round to chase another hare. "It is probably difficult for you to believe,

Megan, that only a short time ago, fifteen years, an American woman could have a conscience in such . . . *robust* condition." The mother did not want to lose the moral of the story, and once it was established that Carrie had had a fine character last they knew, Marcus said they ought to call her and see if she still had. An awkward call.

"I'll do it," said the excellent mother. "I think we even have a number."

"No, that's all right, I'll do it," said the fine father.

And do it he did. It was nearly ten at night over there, and the connection went through to Albi very quickly. Marcus heard his sister through the waves of his returning voice, and their four-minute talk was broken by pauses and hesitations due to the sluggish satellite which scrambled all the nuances that might have been detected in an argument taken up after many years with a sister who lived in Chicago.

"How did she sound, Marcus?"

"Well, you know, it's hard to hear . . ."

"Wasn't she surprised, daddy, I mean to pick up the phone like that, and then without any warning . . ."

"Fact is, she didn't seem *too* surprised, no."

"Well what did she say about me?"

"Oh, she said she was very glad, looked forward to it. I told her, you heard me, that you were on standby and likely you'd turn up around the twentieth. Of course I didn't go into the article. That'll be your problem . . . I wonder what the franc's running?"

Fanny listened to her mother and father talk about what the franc was worth now, what it was worth after World War II, and so on. Everything was settled except Fanny. Suddenly she said sharply, "I must say you take all this very casually. You really run a poor sort of feud. I mean for *me* it was the most unsettling, the most *wrenching* thing in my whole childhood . . . that we would lose Carrie. But at least I thought everybody was . . . grievously hurt and *forever* . . ."

Five

IT was Marcus Foote who had pronounced (with hindsight) that December 31, 1959, was the last time one could take one's bearings by the old Age of Reason rules of thought. From then on there were too many Xs in the equation. The incalculable, the unexpected, the perverse, and what is called the Rush of Events took up too large a part. From then on everything would be a surprise (Black Power, Feminism, Sexual Permissivism), often a nasty surprise, (Vietnam, Watergate, OPEC, Sexual Permissivism). If it had no other use, Marcus said, that December date was a benchmark in this wise: before it, people assumed that serious cultural change took about a generation to be effected. Since then the most rooted restraints are discarded as soon as they are identified. Marriage would be an illustration. Two people no longer feel the need to keep a front, to stay in marriage for fear of ostracism, because of the intimidation of the outside world. The outside world doesn't care. The endurance of a union becomes almost entirely an internal matter and depends upon the fierce sort of *will* Gordon Liddy has—says he has.

Elizabeth and Marcus had been married for thirty-odd years but Elizabeth believed it wouldn't have been another thirty-odd minutes if she ever had said a quarter of what was on her mind. She thought the current injunction to talk everything out, to put it all on the table, was the worst possible advice. With a mind locked, as it seemed, in the pre-1960 scheme of things, she cherished the residual wish to see her children permanently mated, profoundly settled. If sociologists predicted that half of today's unions would end in divorce, why, her children must head for the other half. However, Bud, the older of their two sons, who had been settled four years ago, was becoming unsettled, and Bud said when he heard statistics like that what he found incredible was the fifty percent who hang in.

"You and dad, the Reddishes, the Costellos, the Sidneys, the whole B Street bunch, you're anomalies, the original Noah's Ark. All over America people are splitting like amoebae. You're really bringing up the rear, you know. B Street is not where it's at," he said laughing, goading his mother.

Elizabeth said stiffly, "It does seem that in *your* world with its easy nonbinding living arrangements and the massive *gratification* one assumes to be the happy consequence—it *does* seem that there is little joy in Mudville after all. Everybody drooping around, dropping out, depressed, divorced. It's sometimes difficult to believe you're really onto something."

Bud talked to his mother as though her IQ were sixty-two and she listened to him as though his were. He had been known to say things like "I've got to be happy. If I'm not happy I'm no use to anybody," a sort of aphorism he offered as having universal application.

Bud Foote sounded much less of a fool when he was out

of earshot of a parent. He worked for an architectural firm in Toronto that had awarded him a commendation "for imagination and common sense," which he sent on to his parents to confuse them. He and Laura (Reddish, that was) had flown down for the Labor Day weekend to announce their separation. Laura had stayed with her parents on B Street but the two of them were back and forth ten times in their three-day visit, very civil, even friendly. Elizabeth was exasperated by the divorce. She believed that you might be driven to divorce only when you really hated the other person. Tom was living, unmarried, in Denver, with one Kathy, and that also exasperated her. And Megan at twenty-six would not finish growing up. Elizabeth blamed the times, the mockery in the air, the acid rain.

Elizabeth, daughter of a Lutheran minister, was stiffened by an Old Testament backbone while not acutally believing in an Old Testament God. She was the last one to be taken in by fads. Her oldest friend, however, was Alison Sidney, a handsome, energetic person who greeted the newest youngest ideas with hope, with optimism, and with, from Elizabeth's point of view, a short memory. The women were devoted to each other. Through the years, the back yards conjoining, each confidently had run her household, instructed her children, from an opposing system of beliefs, and in the course of time they were drawn even closer by the unexpectedly dismaying results they both got. The orderly-minded Elizabeth certainly thought her children would grow up, get cracking, and march on, and the nonrepressing Alison certainly thought her children would flower and flourish and create wonderful things.

It is currently a particularly difficult time in American life for middle-aged mothers like Elizabeth or Alison Sidney. When they were themselves brides, they had expected that in due season there would be children, that children once grown there would be weddings and new households followed by grandchildren, the buying of tricycles, the bequeathing of quilts and coffee services. But instead in due season there is a sort of dead stop, a gridlock, an extremely long delay in the time to plant and the time to pluck up that which is planted. These older women are sympathetic— aren't they feminists themselves? And for their sympathy they can expect about ten extra years of worry and uncertainty per child.

Elizabeth did not find herself exasperated by Megan, as she continued to be, on and off, by her sons, but she was unhappy with Megan's prolonged unsatisfying drift, so much so that while her very last recourse would be to suggest that Megan "see somebody," she was about up to this last recourse when the visit to Carrie flew out of the blue. In this visit Elizabeth saw at the very least a diversion for Megan, but in fact she hoped for something more lasting, as a consequence of a general tidying up, an all-round expiation.

Unlike her husband, Elizabeth was not one to enjoy the uses of confession. Rarely had she been heard to say My Fault. In the present family showdown over Carrie, she watched Marcus tapping his chest, tripping around the subject—she herself had long since pieced together to her satisfaction what had caused the blow-up, why Carrie had banished herself—and now she saw Megan become increasingly upset by her father's implication that Carrie had been lost to her for trivial reasons, hardly memorable.

"Loyalties were divided," said Marcus, the equivocator, with philosophical detachment, to his angry weeping daughter, and Fanny suddenly wheeled round at him and said, "What a dopey melodrama!" and stomped out.

"Ach, loyalties are always divided," said the mother into the air, and got up, carefully not stomping because of her back, and followed Megan for a private talk.

With the door closed and sitting on her mother's bed, Megan asked through her tears, "Who was the married man?"

"I'm going to get you a cold cloth," said Elizabeth, and went off to the bathroom to think how much to say. It was a delicate problem. She believed that Marcus, in his monomaniacal pursuit of that congressional seat, thought that Carrie was putting his chances in jeopardy by having herself linked with David Sidney. And out of loyalty to Alison, the last of her loyalties left of that wretched episode, she did not want to let this scandal out, in particular to a member of the younger generation. She had never, in fact, been able to talk about it, certainly not to Alison or Carrie. She had been really bottled up and stoppered, had begun to gain weight and get arthritis and looked a little like a bottle ever since.

She handed Megan the cold cloth and Megan again asked, "Who was the married man?"

"Of course you have to remember that in those days it was not the *custom* to consummate affairs. In all our flirtations we *expected* to be stymied well before we ever got to bed."

Megan waited.

"I always thought it might be David Sidney," said Elizabeth, hedging a little for conscience's sake, and sighing.

"David Sidney? I don't believe it!" said Fanny, and didn't. He was such as improbable choice for philanderer, such a moralizer, that Elizabeth had applied considerable pressure on her own mind to believe it.

"It was a very odd year from start to finish," said Elizabeth, beginning to build a defense. "We were all rather wantonly . . . *lured* away from our own daily preoccupations by that . . . Pied Piper your father . . . We were of course still living on B Street."

We were still living on B Street, the old neighborhood, her sold home. Fanny heard those words as if her mother had said, "Once upon a time there was a little girl," and with a large moan began to cry again. Fussy Fanny who, by any measure, had had the richest of childhoods, who was the only one in her entryway at college to come from a house with the full complement of two original parents, Fanny was a great grown girl awash in a sense of loss.

"It was a very different time, '66, another age," said the mother, pushing on. "You're too young to remember the restricted possibilities we lived with. The church was still a powerful, intimidating factor and a sexual liaison was capable of causing a scandal and a defeat. Even for me it's difficult now to believe what a violation it was then thought to be. And all of us on B Street, the children as well, suspending our ordinary lives to work for the campaign . . . stepping out of character . . . I think the pressure and the excitement affected the judgment of more than one of us . . ."

"Oh, it was a fantastically exciting year," said Fanny, and abruptly, in her mind, came up against a wall. A winning year, her father had won, but she had seemed in some way responsible for letting Carrie go. "Why do you say David Sidney?" she then said crossly.

"Well, really, Megan, I find it strange that you can so *breezily* dismiss probably one of the most gifted men we are ever likely to know. You might ask yourself why Allison has lived with him so long."

"The eighth wonder of the world."

"He's never boring. Marriage to a complicated difficult man has *some* rewards, I can testify to that."

"He's a snob."

"But he's not a reverse snob," snapped Elizabeth. Here she was wrong. All the snobbery that counted on B Street was of the reverse sort.

"I had him in Chaucer and he called me Miss Foote as though he hadn't known me all my life. He's cold."

"He's *formal*. And I might add that his loyalties to your father during the campaign and to Carrie in her fight for tenure are not to be questioned. I've always supposed that *proximity*, the heat and passion of that losing battle with the department—well, it must have carried him away."

"It must be somebody else. I can't believe it's David Sidney," Fanny said sullenly. There were limits to whom she would entertain as Carrie's love.

"I think you have to remember she was the only one amongst us who might be said to be his *peer*, nearly his peer. He said she was that rare thing a true intellectual being. I heard him say it." She paused to reflect and then said, "I think he's mellowed a little. Jews can be prickly. It's understandable."

"Oh, I don't think you can blame the Jews!"

Elizabeth shifted back to Carrie: "When she came back from France . . . she had the six-month leave, and we went out to Logan in a snowstorm to get her, do you remember? She was wearing that green coat. She looked like a duchess. She had gone off looking like an ordinary schoolteacher and she came back looking like a duchess. There was a new style, her hair, a new *carriage*. *Something* changed. And she said Yes, she felt somehow suddenly *unlatched*—it was her word—and she was curious to see what she would make of her release."

"That marvelous velvet coat . . ."

"It was velour. And the first thing we told her, of course, was that your father had filed to enter the primaries. Your father said to her something like 'I count on you to get the Cambridge women stuffing envelopes,' and your dear Carrie, who had always seemed to me to be an awfully *uncritical* sister, really *over* ready to be of service—well, I'll remember her look of detached amusement, of awakening, until the day I die. She didn't say anything. Her brows went up, and she laughed," and Elizabeth's brows went up and she laughed. "And I thought to myself, we've got another Carrie back from what we sent out. I thought it must be a man. But Carrie said it was a woman, that it was just sort of a catalytic thing and she didn't know what would come of it."

"She wasn't telling you that she was . . . um, gay?" Fanny suggested offhandedly, not wanting to jar her mother.

"You mean Lutécie? Oh my dear that's something that never *crossed our minds* . . . It was just not something women *were* in those days."

"Oh, mama, it's just as *normal* a predilection if you take away the cultural pressures," said Fanny in reproval. For herself, she intended to get used to thinking this was true.

"Well, the cultural pressures were definitely heterosexual on B Street anyway. I can't tell you the number of aging swans who were singing that year, ducks and drakes both," said Elizabeth, chortling. She was a chortler, a word Lewis Carroll put together when he crossed chuckle with snort.

"Maybe it was Mr. Costello," said Fanny, doubtfully, but in search of an alternative to David Sidney. And to Lutécie Tavernier.

"Willie? Silent Willie? Good heavens, I can't imagine a

more *uxorious* man. Faye *ruled* him. He was at her beck and call. We thought she had one of those dog whistles that only he could hear. He'd be having a drink with us on the porch and then seem to get a signal and off he'd go. I think he's quite devastated by her death. He's going to sell the factory, I understand." She laughed, bemused, and asked, "What made you think of Will Costello?"

"We used to bump into him a lot, Carrie and I, and I was just wondering if, after all, it might have been by design. I always thought of him as Betsy's grandfather. I must say I have some trouble turning him into a *lover*."

"Well, I don't think you have to bother," said her mother dismissively.

"The Greek vases. It seemed such a coincidence when we'd meet him at the Greek vases. We even met him once at the glass flowers at the Peabody." Fanny's voice tailed off. She took a breath and then said, "You know, mama, I often think of that spring with Carrie, that mad museum binge we went on, two or three afternoons a week, and not just the Fine Arts. I think I learned more . . . was more aesthetically *stretched*, don't you know . . . I know I was very young but I just felt with Carrie that things were coming together . . . you probably don't remember. You'd just begun working at the library."

Elizabeth remembered very well. At the time she had become increasingly—she would not use the abusive word *jealous*. She had put it to herself that Megan was being over-stimulated. A mother was entitled, she had thought, to have misgivings about that sort of *uneven* camaraderie, too intellectually exhausting for a child. What she now saw to be an unreasonable reaction to Megan's infatuation with Carrie's world was the cause of her staying her hand when Carrie decided to leave, of not intervening. It was an act of omission she regretted. She would be glad to get it all behind. "I think you're just the one to be the ambassador," she said warmly, smiling, patting Megan's arm.

"Fifteen years . . . my goodness, we don't know a thing about her," said Fanny, musing.

"Oh, we *hear*. The Sidneys go over often. The Reddishes. They all see Carrie."

"They all see Carrie? What do you mean, they all see Carrie?"

"Well, after all, Megan, why shouldn't they? It isn't *their* feud!"

Six

Fᴀɴɴʏ had planned to take the shuttle back, but now stung by the fact that the ban on Carrie had not been nationwide, and immobilized by jealousy, she stayed the night. Her father, pretending good part, went off to her mother's room and she took his.

Marcus moved warily towards the matrimonial bed, concerned to protect his flanks. He thought of himself as having a mind of quite fertile imagination, had depended upon it countless times and not in vain, but he couldn't seem to jog it into action on this Carrie matter. He had not the smallest doubt the subject would come up. He planned to lie back on his pillow in the dark with his eyes open and see his way through. It seemed to be Elizabeth's intention, however, to do all this truth baring with the light on.

"Now I've told the child *something* about it," said Elizabeth, easing onto her little chintz-covered day couch, cautious about her stiff joints. She was in her nightgown and robe, quite a lot of pale pink, he thought. "And I might just as well say flatly," she continued, in a voice that had the ring of the authorized version, "that I told her the truth. I told her that you were . . . *disturbed* by the possibility of a scandal spoiling your political chances."

It was exactly not it. He had not been disturbed.

Marcus had thoughtfully picked up his pajamas so that he could go off to the bathroom to prepare a response to no matter what she said, but in the event, he so sincerely couldn't imagine what she was talking about that he sat down in confusion on her hard Windsor chair.

"I thought it was sound and fury at the time, and frankly, to this day I'm not persuaded she actually *had* the affair with David," Elizabeth added.

"David," Marcus repeated quietly. "You mean you thought Carrie and David were having an affair?" He found this notion astounding and so far out in left field that it restored his sense of being the aggrieved party.

"I did," Elizabeth said firmly, defying doubt, his and hers. "I remember the reporter—rather smarmy fellow— from the *Herald Traveler* tailing after you all. You had a fit about it and there was nothing you could do, I remember your becoming increasingly agitated."

Marcus looked at his wife in her undulating pink, with her set hair and her set jaw, a woman who didn't know the first thing about horseflesh when it came to sex. He said, "Smarmy, that's the word."

"You were awfully blind about Carrie. I always thought so. It doesn't seem to occur to you that women in the category of sisters, wives, daughters can be seduced by passion, can *succumb*," she said, giving her own self a racy little air retrospectively.

"It's David, Lizzie," he said in a sober tone of correction. "David is just not one of your succumbers, you know."

David was always the weak reed. Elizabeth was reduced to a frown. She crossed her legs carefully.

Marcus was once more confident, but also annoyed to think anybody could cook up such a silly story and then prefer it to the one he'd cooked up. He rose to his feet and with a certain grandeur made what he meant to be his final offer: "*First*, the money was leaking out all over the place. *I* was unnerved. *I* was reprehensible. Second, I confess that I did not see this women's-rights business at all, *then*. I see that she was being shafted by the university *now*. And third, we ought to get one thing straight once and for all. *I* didn't send her packing. She *wanted* to go. She was absolutely infatuated with Lu and she was overjoyed by the idea of a . . . change of venue. Now if, Lizzie, you find this inheritance business insufficiently plausible cause for our rupture, you are right. It was unconscionable." And gripping his pajamas in a strong fist he went off to the bathroom.

From breakfast when his wife dredged the thing up Marcus had spent the day stirring about in his conscience and what amazed him above all was how time had reduced his original transgression—his original attempted and *failed* transgression—to a small trick, to a Rotarian banality. What did it amount to? That he'd gotten heady in the campaign, that when he met Lu he fell hook, line, and sinker, that when he had begun some fumbling inelegant efforts to have her, Carrie cut him off at the pass and carted her away. Fortunately they never spoke about it. At the time he was ready to have it out with her, but due to his obsession the only trade-off that came to mind were words to the effect that he would not interfere with her life—in this case the university's hiring practices—and she should not interfere with his. Really, as he would say to Lizzie of the revised version, unconscionable. The worst of it was that looking from now to then, sitting through a fall afternoon, in beautiful Fenway Park, where he'd sat as a boy countless times with his own father, and in turn with Megan and his own sons—the worst was that he cut such a pawky figure, such a disreputably trivial, subordinary, seamy . . . and at the time he had felt ten feet tall, doubly intoxicating for a shortish man.

On principle, Marcus had not been of a roving nature either before this breach or after, although he was a man who had to say that his own sensual appetite was strong. It would be difficult to find a man who said his own was weak. But he had been born and reared in hierarchical times when there had been a seemliness about misbehavior appropriate to each age. It was in Fenway Park in fact and by coincidence, when he was sixteen or so, that he'd enjoyed a wave of blessed relief because fate had assigned him his own father instead of Bobby Faulkner's, the first, and therefore possibly the most alarming womanizer to come to his attention. He thought he'd heard everything about sex by that time but he hadn't known about the possibility of having a defaulting parent, a humiliating parent. His father, a principal at home as well as at school, could be relied upon to take a strict moral view of human behavior, but at this particular Red Sox game, in the wake of the scandal, his father was ironic, even tender. He spoke in an uncharacteristic roaming tone suggesting clemency. He said in effect that the young begrudge passion in the old, believe the old have had their turn and ought to retire responsibly from the field. He said that from time to time as a man moved along through life he had to impose painful restraints upon himself. He said that Shakespeare gave man seven ages and Freud said there was going to be trouble in every one of them. Marcus could hear him now, see his frowning brow. "A man who believes in God," he had said, "is in a bargaining position. But for people like ourselves the burden is self-control. There is no civilization without self-control."

The conversation haunted Marcus for years, the first and rare sight of the man when he wasn't a father. He had seemed sad, almost confiding, talking on about life, watching the plays, pausing for a hit or a strike, his eyes grazing the field, the bleachers, the sky, never looking at his son. Marcus had blushed to hear his father mention Freud, then to a boy a word which was a smart back-alley reference to sex, the entirely forbidden, purely salacious, and besotting subject. And here was Freud as clean as Shakespeare. At some point in his ruminations, his father said, "You wouldn't want to do it. You wouldn't want to be caught leading a woman you respected through the back doors of hotels."

Marcus had accepted these same terms for a civil life, not counting his brief attempt to do otherwise, and was now sad about it in the same ball park, but not regretful. "Well, the other side won, dad," he said to his father's ghost. "No points at all any more for a man who only sleeps with his wife. Your beloved American know-how has produced the motel. Everybody's got a front door."

Will Costello was sitting quietly by him through this game. Will had a really rare natural gift. He could remain in total silence indefinitely, even preferably. And if called upon he would hear you out. Will was pushing seventy in a couple of years, white-haired since he was forty, long drink of water, didn't jog, didn't really age, kept his counsel, didn't change. People to this day sought him out, tracked him down, cherished him because he was a listener, the only one for miles around.

Marcus pondered on to the bottom of the fourth and then

said to Will, "Well, it seems Megan's going off to see Carrie. Effect a reconciliation . . . bring that sorry business to a close. I guess everybody thought I was a damn fool."

Will considered a moment and said mildly, "I can't think of anybody who didn't."

"Seems Lizzie finds my fit over the money . . . unconvincing," said Marcus, testing this water.

"One silly-assed explanation's as good as another," said Will, who as a listener was a storehouse of stories, and in fact the only one who knew Carrie's.

Marcus resumed pondering. His mother could not have been anybody's model for life's companion, he saw even when he was a boy. Lizzie, on the other hand . . . he thought his own life only really began with Lizzie—a combative, critical nature running to carp, God knows, sometimes—but never banal-minded. Something always fresh about the way she thought. However high he had hoisted himself in his own estimation, it would not have been as high without Lizzie, without Lizzie's expectations. It wasn't in the cards that he'd do as well as he sometimes had. A number of the finest thoughts about marriage thus passed in review through his mind, and when they were sufficiently impressive, he said to himself, Notwithstanding, if I ask myself do I lust for Lizzie, that is clearly farcical. If memory serves the last real full-blown focused lusting I did was for Lu and it took the United States Congress and the Vietnam War together to distract me. However, they did distract me, and moreover, Bud (he was now in his mind addressing his son), I never thought of leaving my wife. His internal dialogue was getting heated and his lips were moving.

"You know when I got back to my practice," he said aloud without warning, without nudging, to Will, who did not jump, "I told Joe Levine I wasn't going to take divorce cases. I'd just do the *pro bono* . . . Well, Jesus God, the last few years it got so much I had to take my share. And now there's suddenly a great surge—people married thirty, forty years . . . they think they've got to get divorced before it's too late, before they're dead. It's as though they want to retrieve their honor, their name, they want to leave with the record straight. I don't know . . . Seems like a crazy travesty on the old sacraments."

"Last chance to be liberated, I suppose," said Will.

"It's the men. You know it's a funny thing but once again the women are left holding the bag. Here are these fellows, reared in the old tradition, buttoned-up, responsible family men, like you and me, sticking through with the ups and downs and then all of a sudden just when you think they're going to head off for Sun City, it's as though they've been *deprogrammed*. But the wives, a lot of times the wives are just not ready for it. They're ashamed. Mostly they're sick with shame. They feel stripped naked. They've been holding everything together this long and they don't know to think differently. You don't have to like them to feel sorry about it. I'll tell you something, I ought to have a diploma in psychiatry. More than one of these old guys—I've suggested what about taking a little *easement*, what about slipping off to the side sometimes, not wrecking the whole . . . oh God no, he's into demolition. He doesn't want a stick standing. You can see the venom building over the years but you don't know why there isn't that . . . detumescence. You're supposed to mellow."

They watched a long fly and then Will said, "Not a lot of mellowing."

Marcus wondered how Will had stood it with Faye. Swallowed her with gin. Sociable nature, always ready for a drink on a weekend afternoon, stay on, and then just when you thought he might have made up his mind to ask for asylum, he'd shamble off back to the barracks. If he had tried to get something going on the side he would have had a tremendous amount of neighborly understanding and cooperation.

"Old Dave," said Will, breaking through.

"Dave?"

"Mellowing."

"Oh, yeah, right."

By the top of the ninth the conversation Marcus was having with himself was getting very querulous. Everbody's out of step except our Albert! That's what they could say about him. He cared about his wife, his children, his *country*, for God's sake. Where did he get off the track?

"Somewhere about the time they began wearing turtlenecks I began getting bored with our side," he announced to Will. Will looked at him, nodded, and seemed to agree. "The young and the neo-young, they stopped being interesting, being, *relevant*. That's when I began to think I was not going to run again."

"I think the turtlenecks were earlier."

"Megan has a friend, you know, who went on to the law school. Well, it seems she came home one day and asked her mother whether the young were boring. One of the lecturers had suggested to the class that the young were boring. They were electrified. She said it went around the school like wildfire. It was a possibility they had never considered!"

"You ought to increase your annual contribution."

"Megan said she found it a refreshing point of view, relieved them of a load of responsibility, don't you know. Megan has a fine ear . . . real quality. I wanted her to go on to the law school. She lacks direction . . . All your kids, they seemed to march right out of the house and into the future."

"They couldn't wait."

And of course naturally Boston lost five to two and all of the afternoon's memory sifting had left Marcus noting ruefully that the grand passion of his life was in retrospect uninteresting in the extreme, that his mind couldn't stay on it, and to give Lizzie pain over it now would be reprehensible and also fatuous.

And that night when Lizzie produced her theory about David Sidney, he was in awe once again how you never know what goes on inside another person's head, what he muses on, what a private preserve it is, what are his rules of evidence, how the evidence need never be subjected to review. It can startle you sometimes what liberties they take in there. When he came out of the bathroom he looked in on Megan and said, "Mother is wrong. I never thought of Carrie's having a love affair. I never thought of a scandal. It would not be right to harbor doubts about Carrie's behavior."

"Carrie's behavior!" she bellowed, and she crossed her arms and wheeled around to show her father her back. He shuffled off mumbling to himself, "I hope this isn't going to be as long as *Hamlet*."

Seven

Fanny woke on Sunday morning, her fury still in place. She sat up in her bed in a lotus position and bellowed, " 'Only connect!' 'Only connect!' I can't connect anything!" She went off to the bathroom where there was no shampoo, no hair conditioner, but where a lot of the family thoughts were collected that weekend, and retrieved for the thousandth time the set piece in her memory of Carrie, a windy spring day when the two of them were sitting on the Rockport rocks throwing bread to the gulls. She had ventured to ask Carrie whether she had ever fallen really in love. At first Carrie didn't answer, and then she looked around at Megan and smiled the happiest smile in the world, her hair flying all over her face and shook her head yes.

"Are you going to get married?"

"I guess not."

"Why?"

"I can't tell you that. It's a secret love."

"Are you *miserable?*" Megan asked, bending around to see Carrie's definitely joyful face. "Why aren't you miserable?"

"Well, I'll tell you why. I was really worried that I would

never know what it was to fall in love, deeply in love . . ."

"So you got that worry off your mind," Megan concluded, and on the spot took it on and had had it ever since. After a decent interval she proceeded, "Does that person love you?"

"You said a mouthful!"

"Well what are you going to do?"

"I don't know. It's a very . . . unexpected love. I wake up every morning surprised. I've told you more than I've told anybody else because I know that if I ask you, you'll never say a word."

"Never."

Fanny remembered referring to "that person" from delicacy, and after this confidence, in a fever of curiosity, pictured him severally as tall and handsome with hobbitlike valor, pacing the terrace of his French chateau in Middle Earth. Or teaching at the university. Or being the governor of Massachusetts. Never did she think that somebody's father on B Street was among the eligibles, and of course never, never that he was a woman. What she had taken to her heart was the knowledge that she herself was Carrie's chosen girl, picked out of everybody, and it gave her ballast through the storm that broke and swept Carrie off, and thereafter. And she had read in Carrie's departure with Mrs. Tavernier a signal flag of the renunciation of the secret love, and took comfort in the belief that she alone could decode it. It made a very unpleasant prospect to have to undo all that.

The breakfast table was a scramble of the Sunday *Times* and the Sunday *Globe* when Fanny came into the kitchen. Marcus looked up and said, "If Pius II had had the bomb and dropped it on the Turkish Empire in order to prevent the fall of Constantinople we would not now have to worry about any emirate on the Arabian peninsula, or Israel, Jordan, Lebanon, Syria, Turkey, Iraq, Iran, and Afghanistan."

Elizabeth said, venturing in the morning light to get all the disagreeable facts out, "Megan, don't you think it would be a good idea to go over to B Street this morning? Because, the fact is Alison's just back from Albi. Titus has been there, at the Printing House, doing some postdoctoral work. It concerns that region, you know, *heresy*, the Albigensian Crusade . . ."

". . . and possibly Romania, Bulgaria, and the southern tier of Soviet Socialist Republics."

"Titus!"

Fanny drew a deep breath, threw up her chin, threw up her arms. It was like wading into a rough surf. Barely onto your feet and you're knocked down again. The ignominy of having that little discardable runt of a Titus complacently —complaisantly—installed in the elegant tremendously coveted salons of that chateau—she had retained the chateau of her original hypotheses and made it do service for the pension—it was the gross taking of her rightful place, a disinheritance of Dickensian dimensions.

"It seems he's becoming recognized for a remarkable scholar. He's like his father," said Elizabeth.

"Oh, well, you can't say finer than that!" Fanny snorted, without a chuckle.

Mother and daughter took the T to B Street. The daughter thought she would crumple at the sight of her old home but did not, in spite of evidence the new owners did not know how to live in it: *shades* instead of glass curtains.

What the Footes meant by B Street was its dead end, where the last several houses on their quarter-acre lots had been built for large-ish middle-class families after the turn of the century, houses that were sold and sold again as the young grew up and moved out. The trees, the shrubs, the ivy covered their hundred architectural embellishments, and the red brick factory that dropped in back behind them, flanking the other bank of their backyard stream, distinguished this comfortable middle-stratum neighborhood from the countless others in the countless small cities of the Northeast. Another point of view is that there was nothing like it.

Alison Sidney had transformed the worst-looking house on the street to the best, which was suitable since she was a kind of professional designer, and also had been an heiress, and in her fifties, now, she still looked both. As she stood by the side of Elizabeth, they seemed the most unmatched pair of friends, turned out by hairdressers with madly clashing inspirations. Elizabeth never looked more like the queen of England than in Alison's living room of Finnish fabrics in purple, raspberry, lavender, Alison matching, Elizabeth the first to say, and say frequently, "Alison pulls off everything in sight." In the middle of this decor from which the crystal and the silver had been removed to higher surfaces, there sat on a mohair throw a seven-month-old baby girl in the traditional pink. She worked out very well.

Fanny had the impression, as they walked in, that whirlwinds were whirling off in other directions, closing doors after them. Handsome Alison assumed a delighted expression, her grey hair rinsed, blow-dried, bounding, as she nodded and marveled over Megan, blue smiling eyes, her grandest feature and cause of the dilemma whether they would be spoiled if she had her skin tightened a little, or not.

"What a godsend you are," she said. "Would you believe

that dear sweet good-natured little pink pug is the cause of a stupendous row? Ook at her. She's *really* into bagels, sucks all the cream cheese and naughty jam off. David's gone to get us all some fresh. Cordelia—*presumably* Cordelia is recovering from a certain *disability* that has been discovered in *me*. Of all people. It seems that, among other failings, I am constitutionally *unable* to talk properly to Annie [who was the pink pug] as in the sentence 'What does oo want?' and that my choice of rhymes when administering the bath is *injudicious*, as in:

> Beanbelly, beanbelly, let's take a swim,
> No, by golly, till the tide comes in."

She was hugging and laughing and settling them and she added, "And Lucia's just putting Jim down. She'll be along."

The Sidneys had gone to the trouble of naming their three children Titus, Cordelia, and Lucia, only to have grandchildren called Annie and Jim. Neither of the young mothers was living with the father of her child, and both returned to B Street and to the assistance of their parents, who could, at the same time, be scrutinized and alas, found defective again and again. Every single one in the house was on every single other's nerves, Annie excepted.

Annie tumbled forward and her lean, long-legged grandmother, in grey slacks, and the rough heavy-knitted cardigan that grandmothers have worn from time immemorial but did not pay $150 for—propped her up again, relocated her bagel, and said, "How do they 'spec' you to hear wight when you don't have one single toof in that whole head?" Then turning to Fanny, she said, "You're going to see *Carrie*. I can't imagine anything that will make her happier.

She's become terribly anxious to return and you may be just the trick. She always wants to know everything about you."

"About me?" Fanny asked, smiling at Alison, loving the sayer of the first mollifying words she'd heard all weekend.

"Oh we've all kept her very well informed. She's got your pictures right above her desk. But of course she hadn't a clue, when I left her Tuesday, that you would be coming over. She'll be thrilled." Alison patted Fanny's knee. She was a great patter in general, patting her husband, and her children, and her life together. Many successful households are run by patters. Now out through a door there streaked into the living room the beautiful body of a naked boy of three who went right for little Annie, gave her a sock, and knocked her over. His mother, reaching him too late, said sternly, "We do not hit people littler than we are." His grandmother, the patter, Annie in one arm, gave his bottom a smack with the others, and said unreasonably but in the queen's clipped English, "Nobody hits anybody," and to her guests, "I'm into behavior modification."

Lucia picked up the now howling Jim. She was not really perturbed by any of the elements of this episode, and by way of hello to Fanny, whom she hadn't seen in at least a couple of years, she said, above the racket of her son, "I hear you're going to Albi. My God, I *envy* you. It's *ages* since I've been there. There's absolutely no place like it! It has an atmosphere that's like a medieval religious order, absolutely *uncanny*, it casts such a spell. People are able to do their work there incredibly well. They've got rules, just like an order. My room was on the top and I could see the bishop's gardens from my little balcony." Lucia, a brown-haired copy of her mother, was Fanny's age, but superior to her in confidence and beauty and general attitude, and had always trod all over her, Fanny felt.

"Oh, I'm just going over on assignment," said Fanny, all but yawning.

Cordelia had entered the room and into a half-meant squabble with Lucia, which was half-addressed to the visitors, in place of actually saying hello to them. The sisters had opposite views on the baby-talking policy. In the middle of it their father came in, back with the bagels, and said, "The parent who does not babble and prattle artlessly with his infant imposes a factitious peerdom upon the relationship." This appeared to mean he was on Lucia's side. He greeted his guests very courteously, the more so that he did not like Elizabeth, and then they all attended to the bagel business.

David, now sixty, was a balding man of medium height, with an air of polish—on his head to the point of shine—who had, over the years, learned to suffer the camaraderie of B Street and sometimes enjoy it. All of his affectional needs were really satisfied by his work, his wife, and their issue. He did not need another soul. At the university he made more than an exacting and rewarding teacher; he went to battle again and again to support the highest standards for the institution against the majority conviction that every standard was an outworn crotchet of a discredited culture. He had been among the earliest advocates for the presence of women on the tenured faculty when it was an unpopular cause, and in '66 was the only member of the Committee on Tenure and Promotion who voted for Carrie. And to this day he did not believe that members of the faculty should sleep with their students, another unpopular cause, standing on that shore like King Canute. Thirty-odd years ago Alison had been his student. He had waited until she graduated, and then had courted her properly. He brought this order, this restraint and wisdom, into his marriage, which kept his wife in a constant nervous fuss. The more satisfied he was to settle quietly and flick off the outsiders, the more agitated became her sociability. Alison was friend-mad.

Notwithstanding his reserve, David was an acute observer. Also he liked being Canute. But there was frequently to his remarks a somewhat mean edge, a permission often allowed himself by the poor loser of his privacy. To Elizabeth he now said, "I hear Laura's walked out."

Elizabeth breathed.

"Do you know, I notice an absolutely new social phenomenon, a new public disllay," David proceeded guilelessly, now, satisfied to have hit a mark. "The *men* are hanging on the *women*. Wherever you go, whatever the age. Quite the reverse of Gertrude hanging on the old king. Quite interesting. A few weeks ago I was in New York—it was one of those threatening summer days, not too hot, and strollers by the thousands were walking up and down Fifth. And then the storm burst and we all scurried into the Metropolitan, and I went off to look at the new Meyer rooms and there were *hordes*, simply hordes of my fellow art lovers packing themselves in. And what I found striking was the number of men in their forties and fifties gazing at, 'sighing like furnace,' and possessively fondling their ladies, while their ladies, many of them, were making some effort to stand free and look at the pictures."

"I wonder at your surprise," said Elizabeth. "I would have said the possessiveness of men was the oldest story alive." David was certainly a possessive husband, and the separation of Laura and Bud was by mutual agreement.

"I haven't made myself clear, I think," David continued unperturbed. "From Homer, from Briseis, women have been trophies, of course. What I noticed in these men was a kind of mournful *gratitude*— a bit sentimental. They don't *boldly* snatch and *coolly* display these days if you take my drift—now."

"And the first Printing House rule," said Lucia to Fanny, " 'No sex.' " She did not apparently feel obliged to bother with her father's drift.

"No sex and no hanging on to," said Cordelia rolling her eyes. She was a lot unlike her namesake.

"Cordelia," said her father evenly, "seems to believe there is no moral dimension to sexual activity, that sex alone, among all interchanges between human beings, is free of that burdensome consideration. Interesting."

"What's really bizarre is that it doesn't work at *all*, at least from what Titus says," Lucia continued, pursuing her own thought, not her father's. "Titus says that everybody there has the most extraordinary interest in the subject."

"Don't be silly," said her father. "That's the way it's supposed to work. Do you know one reason why Eliot admired Baudelaire?" He paused politely but nobody seemed to know one reason. "He said it was because Baudelaire 'was at least able to understand that the sexual act as evil is more dignified, less boring than the natural "life-giving" cheery automatism of the modern world.' " David quoted from memory. He never failed to pass Eliot's observation on to his students.

"Well, I can absolutely assure you that Carrie doesn't think sex is *evil*," said Alison with Jim on her lap, turning pages of a picture book, paying little attention to the content of what anybody was saying.

"Well, I mean I can absolutely assure you that growing

up in this family is a weird experience," said Cordelia to the generality.

"You've got to believe it," contributed Lucia.

"Oh, I don't know. You sound like many other households on a Sunday morning," said Elizabeth, standing up to go, actually believing that she was saying a light and soothing something, and Fanny watched as each member of the family heard her mother suggest that they were ordinary, merely ordinary, and perceptibly they drew their wagons into a circle.

"A pox on that lot," was all Fanny said as she walked off with her mother down the path.

Eight

In the plane back to New York Fanny cried from above Providence to the landing gate at LaGuardia. She had gone up to Boston primed for combat and there found herself under conditions of no adversity at all, and was brought down. It was her habit to be brought down by very little and sometimes nothing. Elizabeth had been the sort of mother who reminded her children from time to time that they were not born on a sidewalk in Calcutta, as she in her own childhood had been ordered to eat her vegetables because of the starving Armenians. It is interesting that although these reminders that American middle-class life is a cornucopia do not immediately and permanently bring people's children around, sharpen their perspective, stiffen them with intention, and send them stoutly forth, they are not abandoned.

Fanny was experiencing dismay in part because her Carrie project had been denied the extravagant response she had thought it entitled to have. She felt she had received a kind of parental rebuff, and that they would resort to any device that might shake her and make her grow up. Well, they did so at the cost of some stature in her eyes. She was disgusted by a family feud with, evidently, no grand principles at stake, no heroic dimension at all, not even an implacable enmity.

That Arcadian B Street was another shocking show. It was not only that all those neighbors beloved in memory failed to turn out in numbers and marvel at her; they seemed, when she heard about them, to sound limp, mildly defeated, unambitious to manage in better style. Fanny had assigned each of them, young and old, an interior sureness to stand in relief against her own uncertainty, but the truth was that after the morning's visit when she put the thought of any one of them under the lens, she felt more distracted than diminished and had to stop crying to think about it. Mr. Costello's intention to sell the thread mill was the rather sorry symbol of them all.

Fanny and her mother had left the Sidney house by the kitchen door in order to cross the back yards to the foot bridge over the millstream. The stream was bordered by a hedgerow of sumac and scrub and every sort of ragged tree, all of it now in high color, not a leaf of it disappointing. The back yards were beautiful that morning, and even the stream itself, which could only be seen from the bridge rail, rushed a little, its load of filth not actually bobbing in front of your nose.

Nonetheless, while Fanny's mind registered with little bursts of pleasure the seasonal charm of the yards, the houses, particularly the white ones, and the red brick of the mill buildings, it was a mind that liked people in its landscape, liked the peasant pulling the cart in *Dutch Rural Scene*. The thread-mill annex, with the cornerstone date 1847, had years ago been converted to studio apartments and Carrie had lived in one with a hide-a-bed for Megan. No Carrie there now. Mr. Costello, always in his office, seven days a week, machine pipes running back and forth across the ceiling, ancient faded advertisements and posters papering the walls, stacks of cartons, file boxes, manuals pushing out from the corners, leaving less and less room for the chairs by the desk—no Mr. Costello there now. They thought surely they'd have caught Mr. Costello.

They did not feel they could drop in on the Reddishes, because of the strain of Bud's divorce. They could not wander up the weedy walk of their own old house to see people who thought it was their own house. Elizabeth, tugged by her daughter's gloomy silence, turned her impatience on other people's children.

"I must say, what those girls call a new *life-style* I call a sorry situation," she said, referring to the two young Sidney mothers. Elizabeth did not like the life-style or the word, equally.

Fanny said nothing. She did not want to betray her own generation and she did not think there was a style. That was it in a nutshell. No style. Whatever those girls went after, they did with energy and resentment. They seemed raw, and without the grace their parents had. Just to take Cordelia, by some counts a terrific model—married in medical school, had the baby her last year, graduated with honors, and then they pull internships, one in Boston, one in Rochester, a million miles apart. Well, they're toughing it out. She said out loud to her mother, "Cordelia's toughing it out. I think you have to admire her." She would not be caught seeming censorious, but in fact she did not admire Cordelia, in her mind greedy, competitive, no fine style about it. Not her father's high style—"high style, as when that men to kinges write." (Chaucer). In fact that baby on the floor was the only one in that family who didn't look grounded. (Fanny).

"I'm very far from admiring somebody who takes on

more responsibilities than she can manage. That little Annie will be the one to pay," said Elizabeth, who did not mind one second being thought censorious.

Fanny had always felt shut out by the Sidney girls, she now sharply recalled. They made her feel that she was socially not of their high achievement, that her family was not really cultivated, not in Europe enough, did not speak French. Even now they seemed impervious to a sense of personal shortcoming, in spite of their, each of them, producing a stranded baby. Lucia had married, had had a child, and divorced in record time, and she told Laura Reddish—who with foresight never did change her name to Foote—that she did not expect a first marriage to work and she guessed she wanted to get it over with. Laura said she had sounded both resigned and despondent. Not a lot of style there.

"I think Lucia is really over the worst of it, now that she's back at school and she'll have a B.A. in June," Fanny said, about the opposite of what she thought.

"I don't know why she should be congratulated for surviving the consequences of all her freely chosen mistakes, a girl with *all those advantages*. And then that little boy, with no father!" Elizabeth tisked without shame. The very notion that with privileges went responsibilities had been out of fashion for fifteen years at least and her mother didn't even notice.

They had turned onto Newbury now, having decided to walk all the way home. Fanny was ready to talk about the Sidneys but wary where her mother would take them.

"What I find very difficult to excuse is such undeflected *self*-regard and an almost total absence of *community* regard," was where Elizabeth was taking them. "Every child brought into the world is entitled to two parents wherever possible, and that ought to be the acknowledged, overriding aim and goal, and especially is this true for people who have themselves had all the benefits of family, education . . . young women like Cordelia, Lucia, with their backgrounds; they ought to be *exemplars* . . ."

"Mama, the way you stack the deck!"

"I don't stack the deck. The very people who should be expected to manage best manage very poorly, it seems *to me.*"

"Well, I suppose I just expect chaos for a while, until women get the hang of it, get the hang of getting *two lives* going," Fanny said in a tone that suggested she herself could live in peace with this transitional period full of personal disasters. Far from true that was. She was made ill by the chaos, but who in the end would turn back, she thought, however much her mind idled through the reigns of Victoria through Edward VII. She had no reverence for its usage of women. It was perfectly wrong, she believed, to have prepared them so poorly. She could never shake off a worry about Mrs. Charles Dickens and whether, if she had recorded her side of the story, all hearts through history would have quite so easily gone out to her husband.

Her mother was not thinking of Mrs. Dickens. She said, after a block, "Carrie would have made a wonderful wife and mother. It is odd. I've known a few single women who, I think, would make wonderful wives and mothers but I don't know any married women about whom I could say the same."

Another block and Fanny said, "You talk as though Cordelia and Lucia were setting some sort of *bad example*, encouraging *family breakdown*. They're just caught up in events the same as anybody else, mama. Missy says there are studies that examine this terrible discrepancy, you know, between the normal home situation of a first-grade child, and the reading books that are full of pictures of the old standard two-parent family, and she says the problem is that they've got to update these books because they're sort of insulting and they're leading to terrible psychological confusion . . ."

"Among the disappointments in my lifetime I'm afraid I have to number the social sciences," Elizabeth pronounced solemnly.

Fanny laughed for the next two blocks.

"Well, it's extremely subtle, the rearing of children," said Elizabeth, after a silence, heading uneasily towards a minor B Street scandal. "Look at those Reddishes. Every one of them a gifted musician. All those children playing away, why, I can remember Peter sitting on a telephone book at the piano playing a little Mozart piece when he was *four years old*. Laura with her violin . . . And Gina. Now how do you account for Gina? Evidently *marked* for a professional flutist. No question of her quality, her dedication. And yet it seems that she was so . . . sexually *precocious*, got herself so *entangled* . . . and in the end has caused such havoc in the graduate school they had to send her off . . . off to Albi, in fact . . . till things cooled down." Elizabeth, who did not usually falter when telling a story, was trying to balance the bad news that even Gina Reddish had been to Albi with the good news that she had brought discredit upon herself and others.

"What do you mean? What havoc?" Fanny asked, holding her mother back, bringing her to a standstill. On top of everything TX used to know Gina Reddish.

"I really don't like to gossip . . ."

"Mama!"

"Well, 'The flesh lusteth contrary to the spirit'—it's the oldest story in the world and you young people flout the rules of self-restraint as if nothing mattered except . . ."

"Mama, the moral is supposed to come at the *end!*"

"Of course you may call me judgmental . . . As I understand it, a member of the faculty, a man in his forties, left his wife and children for her, but in the meantime she was also interested in a fellow student. It's quite complicated. There was another friend, another very gifted young woman, who was having an affair with yet *another* married man on the staff, in the *same department*, and it seems both these women, unsatisfied with the scalps of their elders, began to vie for the young fellow." Elizabeth reviewed at some length the implications of the deplorable and indefensible behavior of that group, Fanny confining herself to the casual comment, "Oh, I'm not surprised. She'd been sleeping around since she was fifteen."

But in fact Fanny once again felt herself under the barrage of every element of envy, the wrong emotion. Gina's careless boldness, her feat of bringing whole households down by the age of twenty-five—it made Fanny almost audibly gasp and was her deplorable and indefensible reaction to her mother's homiletic delivery.

"I cannot blame Hugh and Mary," said Elizabeth sententiously, about to blame Hugh and Mary. "They supervised *every single day* of those children's lives."

"I remember how she'd do anything so she wouldn't look square, look like an overachiever," Fanny said evenly.

"And of course I find those older men foolish and reprehensible."

Fanny herself leaned towards older men.

". . . but I'm not naive enough to think Gina was *seduced* . . ."

"Gina was born street smart." Fanny had wished she were Gina from tenth grade to graduation.

"David believes the fault is wholly with the faculty. He

thinks they ought to take the Hippocratic Oath—'In whatever house I enter, I shall not indulge in sexual activity with the bodies of women or men, free or slave.' "

Fanny always wondered whether she would have liked D. H. Lawrence if she hadn't known her instructor was sleeping with Cathy Watts.

By the time they got home there wasn't much left to be said for B Street, although when Elizabeth drove Fanny out to Logan they had another whack at it. Fanny had said the two Sidney women were beautiful, to be fair.

"They're lucky to look like their mother. Titus favors David."

"Do you know, I think the last time I saw Titus I was just in high school and we went to the Gilbert and Sullivan at Radcliffe. He sang the lead and he was very funny. He played the long-haired romantic poet. Which one is that?"

"It was *Patience* and he was Bunthorne. He made a *marvelous* Bunthorne."

"He was a riot, an absolute riot. Do you think Titus is gay?"

"For God's sake, what is the matter with you!"

Fanny was leaving in the nick of time.

Once back in New York where the question "Do you think he is gay?" was just a routine query, Missy asked Fanny, by way of greeting, as she came through the door, "Well, did they know she was gay?"

"For God's sake, what is the matter with you!" Fanny shot back, taken as much by surprise as Missy was.

Nine

WHEN Fanny called TX to let him know that "Thursday I'm off to Paris on assignment," it seemed to recharge a waning interest in her, and he said he'd take her out to Kennedy. His amusement at her quirky folkways had evidently flagged and he hadn't called her for five days so that it was a wrestle for her to take this initiative. But Fanny's interest in TX had been recharged as well, and for the most unworthy reason. While attracted to him from the beginning, she had been rather more infatuated with herself and her virginal vow until she got a taste of the venery of Gina Reddish. It inspired an amazing lust that scissored through her, an example of that lamentable way one's things get charged with interest when somebody else wants them; even people. She was shocked, badly distracted, and as it fell out, unappeased. TX all full of himself, missing all her signals—"Do you know the rhinoceros is locked in copulation for forty-five minutes?" was as close as he came to the subject—rattling on about "the human face of the multinationals," and his doing a trick on "new thought-oriented teaching," delivered her to her plane untouched, even possibly uncoveted, but laughing. And then she was off.

TX himself hadn't been in Paris for years but he was able to pass along a lot of information—"I have a friend who works for ABC News and they put him up at the George V"—information of that nature. By the time Fanny was actually sitting on the Paris park bench, she was able to reflect that the information that TX had given her, extravagantly immaterial as it was to her present plight, was all she had. She was staying at a student hotel near the Jardin du Luxembourg—*First* had not suggested the George V— where she slept in a large lumpy bed, the room appearing to be the box it came in. The bed was covered by a billowy red counterpane turning the air pink. She was just able to slip crabwise to the window and the washstand, upon which she piled her suitcase, typewriter, rucksack, camera.

Fanny was a plucky girl, slept off her initial panic at the alien nature of a foreign country, and the next day (rainy Saturday) proceeded on foot, with a map, to cross and recross the Seine, making a list of the names of the bridges, exalted, dazzled, happy, unbelieving; looping around the Louvre—closed by a walkout of unannounced duration— over to the cathedral, plotting a course that brought her along the palings of the *ménagerie* of the Jardin des Plantes through which she saw, suddenly, five giant tortoises, immense creatures nestling plate upon plate, in their giant way, and finally arriving at the Gare Austerlitz, exhausted, wet, and hungry, to buy the next day's ticket for Albi. Here she met with the first in a series of reverses. For one, she had never had trouble with French before. France was the first place. And so for two, it took her quite a while to understand from the ticket person, a sort of lady Nazi, that the railroad workers were on strike and in any case there was only a night train to Albi. She then retreated, by Métro, to her quarters, where she learned, for three, from the threadbare clerk with the nonetheless haughty demeanor of his occupation that the American traveler's check, absolutely assured and favored currency in any corner of the world, he would not honor. If she had yen . . .?

That night she sat cross-legged in the middle of her bed, wrapped against chill in her red counterpane, abandoned, starving, tears running down her face from strain, from indignation at being thwarted by the entire French nation, entertaining a host of conspiracy theories, but the next dawn was a misty glorious salmon pink which could be seen by leaning out of the casement far to the right, where at the end of the street was the sky, were the gardens and the palace, and the trees still wet, glinting and steamy. On such a day the problems of money, food, and transportation immediately yielded, or they called off the conspiracy; the railroad workers, for instance, their hearts softened, offering to get up and run the trains on Monday morning.

And so at the crack of the next dawn Fanny was off to her station in a cab driven by a swarthy small man of the Arab persuasion who spoke a clear declamatory French on the subject of the Middle East peace: "I will never go to Camp David, me. The Jews? The Jews? I get along fine with the Jews. We all live together very peacefully in my quarter. No trouble at all. Sadat! He wants a short life! No true Arab can possibly forgive him . . ."

"Don't you think it was the *first step* . . .?" asked in a weak voice in a prepared sentence the relatively strapping girl passenger in the back.

"Is not possible! you think *perfidy* is the first step? You experience an admiration for perfidy?" And so on, to the station, where Fanny pulled her gear out, paid her fare, and said to him very sternly, "You are altogether wrong. You *must* go back to Camp David!" And went off quickly through the milling crowd.

In the Gare Austerlitz she lost her breath at the sight of the great and noble trains, rising one after the other at the starting gates, out of old English movies, out of Monet paintings. She found the placard announcing her train, the most imposing placard of them all, and she read the names Orléans, Limoges, Brive-La-Gaillarde, Souillac, Gourdon, Cahors, Montauban, Toulouse, Narbonne, *Barcelona* (a *frontier*—Michael Redgrave in . . .), and she put down her stuff and copied the list. She had the luck of a window seat in a quiet elegant compartment and wished she were wearing her white silk shirtwaist, similar to the one in *Casablanca*, regretted she did not look as fine as the train. She wore jeans; a statement but not on her a flattering statement. She was in fact not lean enough, not angular, had the wrong bones, lacked the languor. She simply was not languid, her cross.

Fanny hoped the trip would last forever and it did. To begin with, she was transported, on a roadbed so smooth that she scarcely felt the motion of the train, so un-American. The train glided through several miles of industrial suburbs south into the Beauce, countless miles of flat market gardens laid out in large squares as far as one could see—industrial agriculture, no villages, no peasants. Finally the city of Orléans, where she thought hard about The Maid. More varied countryside and then Limoges, not at all a fragile and delicate city, but ranging with factories, chimney stacks, and high rises. Fanny applied her mind to teacups and dinner plates, probably Wedgwood. The land began to change to foothills and valleys with even castles here and there, and after more hours to sterner mountain-

ous regions where the train was abruptly sucked into black
tunnel after black tunnel. It was six hours to Toulouse,
Fanny's stop. She dozed, ate her sandwiches, drank her
wine, reviewed her material on Albi, difficult to come by,
a city in south central France not near any known locations
like Provence, Lourdes, Biarritz. A lot of history had been
written about it but not really recent, not much beyond
1480 in fact. By the time she reached Toulouse she was no
longer enthusiastic about travel. Then followed the confusion of the station, and another hour on the bus to Albi,
and the end of the world's longest day.

It was dark when Fanny got out of the taxi and rang at
the wrong house. She seemed to have said 82, rue de la
Temporalité, instead of 92.

Finally, 92. She knocked. The door was opened by a servant or a widow who also thought she had come to the
wrong house, but signaled her to remain in the vestibule, to
stand on the sisal mat, while she went off to see.

Fatigue had robbed Fanny of her aplomb and her appearance, which in the morning had begun as ordinary anti-
preppy might well have misled a servant or a widow of the
old world to believe that she belonged at the back door.
Fanny waited obediently on the sisal mat. The vestibule
was not large. It was oval and had a marble floor, very elegant, and a winding stairway with a railing of polished
brass. There was a table with a surface just wide enough to
hold a faience bowl filled with cut flowers. For the first
moments she was numb with nervous fatigue but when
nobody came, when there was no sound of the intention to
deal with her, she became indignant and was just going to
make a move off her sisal mat when someone could be heard
upstairs, bounding out from wherever, taking the steps at
the gallop, and in a second there was the almost familiar

smiling shiny face of Titus Sidney—looking ridiculous, like a balding boy, with his slight frame, and wearing glasses, tweed jacket, tie, and royal blue sneakers. He reached for her hand to give it a good shake, and said, "I'm *sorry*, my dear *Megan*. Mme Maury *said* you were here, *thought* you must be wanting the youth hostel across the road. How *uncivil* we must . . . Come in, come in!" and he took the suitcase and the typewriter, and led her up the stairs, talking excitedly.

"Carrie didn't *expect* you till the mid week. She's going to be *desolated*—in France they desolate awfully easily. I know which room she means you're to have. It rises right above the river, too high to get a good look at the raw sewage empty out of the drainpipes, although you can catch a glimpse of the white belly of a dead fish when the sun's right. Grand view of the palace gardens." At the landing he put her luggage down abruptly, turned to her, gave her hand another good shake, and the lights went out. He flicked a switch and they went on again, and he led her down a corridor, opened a door, and efficient, brisk, enthusiastic, flicked its lights on in the prettiest room, put the bags down, went to the window and pulled the long green-printed draperies fiercely to each side, opened the glass doors to a small balcony and the night, led her back out of the room and down two doors for the WC, next one for the tub.

"Well," he said happily, "you look dead. Dinner's at eight. You've got an hour. We only dress for dinner," and he offered his hand again so as to be off.

"Oh, good God! Don't go! Wait a minute," said Fanny, knocking her clogs off, and she turned to clutch Titus, now two inches taller. Immediately he sat down on her bed. "What do you mean, dress for dinner?" she asked.

"Well, you know your aunt. She lives a regulated life
. . . so of course, we live a regulated life."

"I really don't know her. I don't know what you mean. I
haven't seen her since I was twelve."

He studied her for a moment and said, "That's right."
And then with a dart of his eyes to the neighborhood of her
hips, he said, "Well, I think it would be fair to characterize
her as a person who doesn't like *anything* to hang out."

"What do you mean? No jeans?"

"Not for dinner."

"I don't believe it!"

"Well, now, if I had to *defend* her on this matter I would
say that she was truly embarrassed by what she sees as,
well, an affected insouciance . . . pretensions to a democratic alliance with the *working classes*, that sort of thing. It
seems to remind her of Marie Antoinette carrying a milk
pail. I don't think she would mind somebody who was a
genuine unemployed laborer. Ah! And speaking of which,
here he *is!* A genuine unemployed laborer. Alain Grossepatte! Alain, I would like you to meet Megan Foote, the
niece." Titus said this with a flourish as though he'd pulled
Megan from his sleeve.

There in the doorway stood a hulking man with unruly
dark hair, unruly black brows, wearing a black turtleneck
sweater and a tan corduroy suit. They shook hands and
Titus said to Fanny, "Alain has come down from Paris to
study us. We are his *subjects.* We are his discrete colony of
English-speaking expatriates. We're the substance of his
doctoral dissertation. He'll like you."

And to Alain, "Definitely, you'll enjoy the change."

And then back to Fanny, "He's a sociologist and his topic
has to do with the adaptation, with the change in habits and
thinking patterns of foreign . . . what the hell is the title of

your topic?" And then before Alain could answer, he continued, "It's *amazing* the sort of thing that interests the social scientists, and he's got this American girl friend who's studying marriage patterns among French peasants in the mountain communities around here. It seems the young women always want to marry a fellow lower down on the mountain. Interesting, isn't it? Everybody else wants to marry up!"

And then back to Alain, "Well, I was explaining to our new guest that Mademoiselle was particular about appearance. You almost starved to death, didn't you, old boy?"

And to Fanny, "He'd blown his last three hundred francs on American Levi's just before he came down, and there was no dinner until he could borrow for the suit. I own two-thirds of the suit, with of course no allowance for depreciation."

"It seems like an awful intrusion into one's personal . . . I wonder why you stand for it?" Fanny said, laughing.

"He got hungry, that's all," said Titus.

Fanny was always hungry. She opened her suitcase to see what the skirts looked like after three days, and turned to the men dismayed.

"Do not derange yourself," said Alain, who spoke an enthusiastic English. "There is a kinship factor. I do not think an aunt denies *family*. That is a cross-cultural phenomenon. She will provide."

"She won't be back till Wednesday," said Titus. "She went off with Berg the Filmmaker. He came to Albi for the color. He wanted to shoot a red town. Well, would you believe it's the wrong red? Doesn't suit the erotic mood of his material? And so Carrie's gone off with him to find a better shade of red. She doesn't even like him but she was restless—waiting *for you*. I think we should eat in the kitchen tonight. Tell Mme Maury we'll eat in the kitchen," he said to Alain. "She hates it when we eat in the kitchen," he said to Fanny, with a look of satisfaction.

"You tell her," said Alain. "And Mme T. will know of her arrival. Certainly she will expect the courtesy of a greeting. But she is only the figurehead. It is Mademoiselle who is the controlling spirit, makes the success. She wings the cloot."

"Clout," said Titus.

"Clout. Madame is merely a carved saint," said Alain.

"Some saint!" said Titus.

"A front woman," Alain added.

"The beard," said Titus, now grinning and even dancing a little, and Alain, kept up-to-date in the English language by Titus, laughed and slapped his thigh.

"You see, I really don't know these people," said Fanny back to her own concerns, "my aunt, and Mrs. Tavernier, and I haven't the least idea what kind of place this is . . ."

"Now that is precisely the question I pose to myself," said Alain, "but I am not yet satisfied to find the proper category."

"I help him all I can," said Titus, grinning. "I'll help you."

Ten

THE old rosy pink city of Albi extends above both sides of the escarped Tarn and is so deep in color that it seems to tint the clouds. What is ironic is that if its medieval center is rescued and preserved it may be as a consequence of the most modern free-wheeling of social trends. Young couples, both man and woman working, choosing dogs instead of children, are buying and restoring the decaying brick and half-timber buildings. Other people's posterity will owe them a lot. An impassioned Safeguard our Heritage Society, Lutécie Tavernier an active member, is dedicated to the preservation of hard-core Vieil-Alby, and has been ambitious to compete with Miami Beach and Las Vegas for international congresses, so far with only modest success. But three times they've gotten the ophthamologists. On the last of these occasions Lutécie, busy keeping track of her many organs, was able to secure an examination by a man from the Mass Eye and Ear. He said she needed glasses.

Albi's history has been as red as its brick. In the eleventh through thirteenth centuries there was a heresy, the Cathar heresy, that spread from Bulgaria across nothern Italy and southern France and into Spain. These heretics seem to have lived amicably alongside the orthodox Christians (and also the Jews) for several generations. Nonetheless the king of France and the pope felt it incumbent to wipe them out and they preached a crusade to this end. The armies of nothern knights descended to the South in waves, laid siege, starved out, and otherwise slaughtered the wise and the foolish inhabitants equally, across an extensive territory in a crusade to which Albi has almost haphazardly lent its name: the Albigensian Crusade. Simon de Montfort was the general put in charge of this crusade. He is said to have told his knights (and this may be a libel on his name), "Kill them all. God will recognize His own." In any case, this warring atmosphere inspired the building of the brick fortress cathedral of Ste Cecilia, accessible to the flock only by a single long flight of steep stone stairs, and a bishop's fortress palace, presently guarding the paintings of Toulouse-Lautrec.

The Printing House was restored in the same pink brick. It had a claim to being first established before 1500 by an itinerant artisan from Lyon who carried on his back the new movable type, and who struck luck by coming to the attention of the bishop, a man immediately won over to the idea of the virtually endless replication of his thoughts. And not just this bishop. And not just bishops. So through the centuries the printing establishment was said to have flourished. By the end of the nineteenth century, however, it fell to the invention of the linotype and sometime thereafter passed into its pension phase under the direction of a branch of Lutécie Tavernier's family. There was an American historian staying there now who was studying the history of printing—and Alain was studying her. Alain said to Fanny, "She believes sometime in this place you can smell still the ink. I don't smell. He smells," he added with a nod at Titus.

"It's how you tell a historian," said Titus.

They were sitting in the large blue, green, and oyster white tiled kitchen at one end of a long soft-wood table, its edges covered with graffiti incised by the fingernails of restless servants of an earlier era. Titus had said in French to Mme Maury, "Let me introduce you to another Mlle Foote, *a niece*. She will be staying with us for two weeks." Mme Maury, expressionless, made a gutteral noise.

"That is not a French grunt," said Titus to Fanny. "It is a grunt in the regional Occitan dialect. You are an event. Madame does not like events. Do you know that your aunt is one of the few American scholars proficient in the Provençal language?"

"No, I didn't."

"She's been invaluable to me. At the time she left she was the only one in the whole United States who was prepared to teach it. And she couldn't get a job. And in fact it's entirely possible from that day until I turned up no American wanted to learn it. Now two of us know it. It renders us both unemployable. We're thinking of going home to whip up a new cult. We understand they're short one cult."

Evidently Fanny had arrived at the Printing House at the very moment when its future had been put in doubt. Carrie was the cornerstone and she was upheaving, wondering whether they mustn't all head back to America. This was an unwelcome and disturbing notion to Lutécie and to many of the other residents who had lived there for some time, and they were covertly lining up against her, and meanwhile walking on eggs, hoping the impulse would subside. Titus had thought that Lutécie would grab at the chance to head right back to Thirty-seventh Street. She was such a devoted New Yorker. Only a quirk of fate had shipped her off to Albi.

"The inheritance of this place turned up just at the time she was needing space," said Titus. "I use the California meaning of the word."

Alain, who designed *U*, *V*, and *W* curves, had a section of his thesis computing anxiety levels achieved by expatriates proposing to return to America. He applied this to Lutécie: "Anxiety increases proportionate to the length of time they have been away," he said.

"Well, that's going to be another exciting chapter," said Titus.

"Is very very difficult to return to the States after many years," said Alain sternly. "Family, hometown village, the tradition, the religion—no support systems. You want to go home, no home."

Titus, who was himself having trouble going home, was not going to give Alain data for his graphs. He said, "The reason Lutécie doesn't want to go back is because of the weather. There are a lot of overcast skies in Albi and she looks better under them. They suit her. They take twenty years off, she believes. As a matter of fact, there are a lot of impoverished old people around here and the question is do they stay because they're vain and look younger, or because they're too poor to move. What do you think, Alain?" But Alain didn't bite.

Fanny lay in her bed that night, the shutters closed, the room black, surprised again as in Paris by how enveloping and un-Posturepedic was French bedding. She thought she was as happy as she had been in her adult life (five to seven years). She had in three days seen so much, all French, all foreign, and she thought, "I smell it. I must be an historian." And there were overcast skies when she woke up in

the morning, beautiful French overcast skies and rain coming down from them. She woke in the same condition of
exultation, found her room infinitely engaging, put all her
things in its wardrobe, on its tables, wiping out Lucia, and
thinking how odd it was that Titus belonged to that handsome family. She transferred her flowers from a tooth glass
to a water pitcher—Alain had taken a fistful from a bowl
downstairs and handed them to her—and so, she saw, it
had been after all the smell of foreign flowers and not a sign
from Clio the muse.

Titus and Alain, incessant talkers, took the day off from
whatever it was they claimed to be doing, trotting her
through the Printing House and then around the town.
Whatever she looked at, she was assured it was not at its
best. She was directed to imagine Madame (that is, Lutécie
Tavernier) sitting on the grass in a great straw hat and yards
of flowery gauze, with her little grandson, putting chestnuts into a bucket. "He and Carrie are probably the only
ones to see her in direct sunlight," said Titus. All that
Fanny saw through the wet window however was a large
grass square in the shape of a cloister formed by the wings
of the building and a stone wall at the escarpment edge.
Four dripping chestnut trees were a dull green, not quite
yet turning.

She thought the Printing House would have been a grand
place for a child to visit if it didn't break its neck. There
were at least two circular staircases, a maze of narrow halls
with uneven floors, and everywhere they went, the lights
went out and they groped. In a little drawing room there
was a golden harp, four white papier-mâché doves resting
on its top, with real feathers. A child would love it. The
public rooms were rather elegant and understated, just a

few bibelots. Almost underfurnished, Titus said, which was very unusual in France. Lutécie was the one with the eye, he said. When Titus had first come to the Printing House Lutécie's old mother was still alive, and the six-year-old grandson was there while its father was negotiating one of his divorces.

"The old mother was ninety-one," said Titus. "Everybody who met her would say, 'Ninety-one! My, my, you look at least ten years younger!' And the old lady would snap, 'That's because I never indulge myself!' and she'd give an absolutely killing look at Lutécie, which wasn't justified, if you want to know. By using precisely the opposite method Lutécie looks nothing like her age. In the lamplight she looks almost like a girl. That's why you're going to meet her in the lamplight." Fanny had been invited to tea at six.

They had been walking for a long while through the narrow streets, between tilting half-timbered houses, and Fanny's attention kept scattering and refocusing on what she was seeing and what she was hearing. The men were running on about Lutécie. Sometimes the talk fell pell-mell on her head with the rain. They crossed to the middle of the old stone bridge and leaned on the wet parapet, and saw the whole red town rising on the palisade, saw the Printing House with the chestnuts looking very green.

Alain said, "She had many men once, Mme T."

"She came very late to an appreciation of women," Titus said ironically.

"All American women are feminists. Is true?"

"After she passed fifty she wanted to give up men, but who to fill the gap? That's when she discovered women," said Titus. "She now believes she was always a feminist. Is true. I myself find it difficult to see a direct connection. I think her gifts lie elsewhere. There is something catalytic about her. She's a sort of professional *inspirer*. You do seem to find yourself *charged up*."

"Is very funny, no, the feminism? She renounces men. Ah, but they do not renounce her," contributed Alain.

"That's true. She couldn't peel them off," said Titus. "The more adamant she, the more ardent they. At first she was looking for a temporary change of scene. But where? What wasn't New York was salt mines. And then providentially, along comes the inheritance and Carrie, and off they sail on the *France*. Their stateroom was filled with the regulation flowers, champagne, and suitors who promised to follow, which they did. There are still some survivors."

There came a time in the afternoon when Fanny did not want to hear another blessed word. In fact she wanted to talk, put in her own two sous, but it seemed difficult for either Titus or Alain to be interested to know anything about her, the outsider. At last she said, anxious and insistent, "Listen, I've got to tell you this and I'm not going to move another inch." She was standing over a grating near the postcards in the cathedral, tears in her eyes. The cathedral was astonishing, remarkable beyond description, but Titus had been remarking and describing for an hour. The intensely reactive Fanny was used up. Heat was billowing from the grating and the tears were in gratitude for somebody's turning it on.

"Now listen, I'm called *Fanny*. I would like to be called *Fanny*."

This announcement brought about thirty seconds of uncertain attention ("Fanny?" "Fanny." "Not Megan?" "No." "Fanny."), then confused silence. They didn't think this was what she wanted to say and waited, politely.

"Well, I write. I mean I plan to write. I needed a short

name. I have the longest name . . . I wanted a name that
could be remembered . . . Fanny Foote, I thought . . ."
  They stayed silent, taking this as an introduction to what
she had on her mind.
  "Actually the fact is I work for a magazine called *First*.
I don't know whether you know it? It's a feminist magazine
in New York, extremely successful . . ."
  She waited for some response, confused in her turn by
their seeming resolute uninterest in her. After a long
moment Titus said, definitively and sounding like his
father, "No way. You can't write about them."
  Fanny flushed and Alain, confused by the English, feeling his way, hung a great protective arm around her neck
while she stood eye to eye with Titus and said, evenly,
"You think I intend to be underhanded?"
  "I think a good journalist goes after a story."
  "I don't know that ruthlessness is the measure of quality
in *my* field. Perhaps it is in yours," she said, biting her
words. She had not really thought of herself as a journalist.
She had not previously perceived her vocation as a writer.
The more she wished to appear forthright, the more she felt
driven to dissemble. She did not like Titus.
  Alain, who caught up with the drift, said, "But of course.
How can she estimate the private quality that is the ambiance of l'Imprimerie? She does not know the aunt. She does
not know Madame. She heard this morning the piano, she
heard the cello, she hears typewriters. But she sees nobody.
She looks through the window and there is no Madame
cleaning up chestnuts," and turning first to Titus and then
to Fanny, he wound up, "She is not without pity. You are
not without pity. Let's get a drink."
  "Is mean 'ruthless,' " said Titus.
  Fanny really liked Alain.

Eleven

NEW Yorker to the bone though she might be, Lutécie Tavernier was actually born in Toulouse, a city only seventy-five kilometers away, and she had never once been back to visit. She had been brought to America as a child of nine just after the Great War, when her father, a violist, joined the Metropolitan Opera Orchestra. She remembers to this day, with a little *frisson*, walking down the gangplank into the sunshine of the wharf, and feeling herself embrace her new country with her whole heart, flappers to Mary Pickford. Immediate hundred-percent-American girl, she planned to be a star, and could not wait to grow up and betray the French bourgeois values of her family. At thirteen she was taken for eighteen. Every schoolday morning after kissing her *maman* good-bye, she would pop into the dark of the vestibule, and with four safety pins and two strings, lower her skirt beneath her middy blouse to a vampish length, and sail off into the world which was Fulton Street, Brooklyn. At eighteen she eloped to Greenwich, Connecticut, with the forty-plus-year-old famous tenor

Tavernier. Now at sixty-eight she could not remember the exact year he died.

At a few minutes before six on this present evening, more or less faithful Bennie Jones was in attendance in Lutécie's corner of the Printing House drawing room, all the draperies pulled. Lutécie was wearing a black wool caftan with a neckpiece of amber that looked like the large Syrian apricots that are strung on hemp and can sometimes be found in Quincy Market, Boston, and presumably Syria. She had a fine brow, with fair hair drawn to the back of her head and held by a gold clip. She wore earrings of filigreed gold, rings on her fingers, and bracelets that clattered up and down her arm. Settled on the sofa in a good dim light she said, "Bennie, you aren't the only unexpected visitor. You remember Marcus Foote? His daughter has turned up. She arrived last night. We didn't think she was due until Wednesday or Thursday. Carrie will be mad as the devil not to have been here."

Lutécie was herself pleased. She preferred to have a free hand in the direction of first impressions.

"Ah," said Benedict Jones. It was an equivocal sound that did not commit him to interest in the other new guest.

"You didn't like Marcus Foote," said Lutécie. She jiggled her toeless mule impatiently. She found Bennie cagey about people. It was impossible to get a good deconstructive chat going. His only curiosity was in places and things.

"I didn't think about him at all," said Bennie. "I don't to this day." Their tea was English whisky and he was content to let the subject die.

Lutécie lifted her chin and gave Bennie a squint, marveling at his slide into happy decrepitude. He had the usual bemused smile on his face as he looked off into a dreamy nothing, but now there was a black hole where a top front tooth was missing. Ludicrous. She thought his mind was going. Twenty years ago he had been a tall, lean man, handsome, rich as Croesus, with frayed cuffs which she had thought of as giving just the right touch of self-forgetting in a world of egomaniacs.

"You know, since Carrie's heard about the girl's coming, she's been beside herself," said Lutécie. It was a calm observation. "I suppose you might say Carrie has lived a thwarted life. She would have wanted a child." Along the way, Lutécie had had one child, who was now a twice divorced air-force colonel in Omaha, Nebraska. Disappointing.

"Ho, now, Carrie? I see her as making a smashing success of things," said Bennie, and he smiled untroubled by the gap from the missing tooth, and he shifted in his too small chair, which creaked. He was still the long gangly man but had added in the middle a notable stomach. He wore the jacket from one old suit and the pants from another.

"For God's sake we've got to find you a tooth," said Lutécie, impatient.

In the stories about Lutécie's lovers, Benedict Jones was the one identified roughly as a Greek shipping magnate. In fact he was a scion of a family of ship chandlers from Portsmouth, New Hampshire. In the old days he had wandered the world selling ship fittings and the extended territory suited him, suited his vagabond nature and his antiquarian interests. Vagabond, in old English statutes, is "such as wake on the night and sleep on the day, and haunt customable taverns and alehouses, and rout about." Lutécie waked on the night and slept on the day and it was her timetable that Bennie, when in the course of decades he found him-

self stranded in New York City, had found congenial. It
was the sixties. He was always there to say good-night to
her friends. But he was such a laconic sort of man that a lot
had to be made up about him.

Lutécie had been reclining on her sofa in a pose similar
to the one struck by the young Empress Pauline, but now
she elbowed herself to an upright thinking position and
said, "You know, Bennie, you haven't seen Carrie for a
while, but lately she's been taken by some strange *obsession*.
I suppose it's what happens. You find yourself approaching
fifty, having produced no descendants, no lien on the
future—but at least she can point to the Printing House as
her own *considerable* accomplishment . . ." Here she paused
for Bennie to say, "Well, Lu, you had a hand in that too, of
course," but Bennie said instead, "She's got her work."

"*Absolutely*. But she can't live on it, and the Printing
House underwrites it beautifully. Well, and now what do
you think? Suddenly and after all these years, she wants to
go home! She wants to go lumbering *back* to America, like
a dying *elephant*, to the great hunting ground from which
no hunter ever returns. Morbid. And if I ask her why, she
says America *touches* her. She's got this terrible longing to
be there in its *dark days*. And I'll tell you what I think
started it. We had an awful sort of *Delphic sibyl* here a few
years ago. She was working for the Club of Rome. And all
we heard about was *finite resources*, the end of *fossil fuel* . . .
Great big muscle-y woman belonged right up there on the
Sistine ceiling. You know Carrie's always had a terribly
active social conscience. It's really a very nice quality . . .
And now there's *Alain*—my God, what we needed *him* for!
You met him. He's that great teddy bear who's come down
from Paris to *study* us. And *he* is investigating our *identity*.
They talk for hours about it. It seems we all have the most

acute American identity. And now with young Megan coming . . . Well, that certainly means a reconciliation with her family . . .

"Listen Bennie, nobody's a more wholehearted New Yorker than *I, you* know that. But we've made a bit of Madison and Thirty-seventh right here without the hassle, and with her passion for poking about every hill for a heretic, here she is, no air fares, all the time in the world for her Provençal mania."

"A lot of people think time is running out," said Bennie philosophically.

Now it was that Fanny advanced towards them uncertainly from the dusk of the doorway, and Lutécie, catching sight of an unfamiliar good-sized girl, flung out an arm of welcome to her and said with such grand authority, "You're *Megan*," that Fanny, who had prepared to introduce herself as Fanny, said, craven—and she thought even with a tremor—"Yes I am," and crossed the room to take the hand held out to her and pressed the fingers carefully, all their rings clicking but not pinching.

"Let me *see* you," said Lutécie, sounding pleased as can be, and giving her a good sweeping inspection. "You don't look like your father," she said firmly.

"Oh, well, I . . ."

"And you don't look like your mother!" she added in a little trill of triumph.

Fanny made an apologetic murmur. She was disconcerted by the youth of this old woman.

Lutécie said, "I want you to meet our dear devoted friend Benedict Jones. He's just stopped for the night. He's fallen off a donkey and lost his tooth. He tripped on his own legs. They were too long. We're having whisky. No tea, Bennie, we'll give her whisky for courage."

Bennie had gotten up to greet Fanny, and he now gave her shoulder a clap of support and said, "You look corking, a lot like your aunt Caroline," and went over to pour the whisky. Lutécie brought out his protective feelings for other people.

"She doesn't look at all like Caroline," said Lutécie. The whisky burnt Fanny's throat and restored her amour propre. She asked Bennie where he'd been riding a donkey.

"In the Cévennes," Lutécie answered for him. "He led a group of sixteen British trekkers on donkeys for ten days in the *Cévennes* following the route Robert Louis Stevenson took a hundred years ago. Stevenson wrote a book about it."

"Oh, I know the book. I haven't read . . ."

"You're much bigger than the donkey, Bennie. It would make more sense if the donkey fell and lost *his* tooth," Lutécie observed. She turned to Fanny, whose appearance she examined head to toe and corrected, and said, "Well, I hear the boys showed you the sights today. What did you think of them?"

Fanny thought, she's cutting off my hair, but the whisky coursing through, she said quite passionately, "You know, I've never been to *Europe* before, and I've longed to see *France* above all, and I *did* of course see the cathedral in Paris, but when I walked through the doors of Ste Cecilia *so unprepared*, I . . ."

"I mean the boys. What do you think of them?" Lutécie asked.

With just a slight pause Fanny said, "The men? I loved them. They're very funny. We laughed our heads off."

"You're quite right," said Lutécie without a slight pause. "There's nothing tackier than hearing elderly women refer to grown men as 'the boys.' It's never too early to say *men*.

It might even encourage a maturing that is so often want-ing. It's why I like you, Bennie. There's always been some-thing all grown-up about you."

Bennie laughed and the tooth hole gaped. He said to Fanny, "I knew your father when he rescued Lu, got this place for her."

"In point of fact, your Aunt *Carrie* rescued me. She had a tremendous sense of adventure. She made the thing work," said Lutécie, noble and generous. For the rest, she spoke in a self-mocking way that was meant to be engaging but not convincing. "Nobody who knew me could have believed it possible that I'd be a successful transplant—nobody. That I would flee the cultural center of the world, go off to possibly the most remote, though quite beautiful, town in Europe . . . They thought I would flee right back. Ah, but I was doughty, wasn't I, Ben?"

"It was Carrie who was doughty," said Bennie.

Abruptly Lutécie turned her full attention to Fanny and said, "I want to hear *all* about you," and waited with an attentive smile.

Fanny, in confusion, could not think of one thing to say.

Lutécie then said in a kind and encouraging way, "Well, are you a virgin?" And added, "I suppose it's one of those questions they don't ask any more."

"They never asked that," said Bennie.

"Yes and no," said Fanny.

"Well, just a minute now, Bennie. Do you imply that it is a frivolous and intrusive question?"

"I'll say it outright."

Lutécie suddenly laughed, her disarming laugh. She said, "In fact it was *not* frivolous. I was just taking the mea-sure of the times. Do you know what Junie told me? He said that when Emerson visited London somebody swore to him very solemnly that there were only five virgins (he was referring solely to men) in the *whole* of England and he could *name* them. Emerson was very shocked. Junie says in Emerson's day the English thought American society was abnormally puritanical, and now suddenly today it's become decadent and dispirited. There aren't *even* five virgins, *he* thinks. So you see, Bennie, I was taking a poll. Now *Carrie* thinks it's become decadent and dispirited by *mistake.* I suspect she believes if she were to return home she could revive the sense of moral fineness. I detect that sneaking reformist hope."

Lutécie with this seeming prattle was laying out her very deep concern that she was going to be folded up and carted back, forced to return to an American scene which seemed to her to have undergone a very vulgar conversion since her day. In her day there was an art of unconventional living and she was widely admired as a mistress of it. She knew its nuances. Now, in the wink of an eye, there wasn't a nuance left. The very word *sex* had lost its raciness. Her personal history was eclipsed, the subtlety shouted down. It had her gloomily counting virgins.

Lutécie did not want to return to America and there were several longtime residents of the Printing House, Junie Waterman their ringleader, who were also understandably made anxious by rumors of the possible dismantling of their home. It was Junie Waterman who now came out of the shadows and to the little group announced, "If Carrie goes back there'll be six." He was referring to the virgin count.

Fanny was introduced to him and to his wife, Maryann. They were a notably handsome couple, he in his sixties, she, impossible to guess. Maryann spoke warmly to Fanny, assuring her that she and Junie just could not wait to meet her, but Junie seemed able to wait indefinitely. He had immediately turned to Bennie, whom he hadn't seen in some time, and proclaimed what a bounty it was to live this far distance (Albi) from the practices of the world he wrote about (NYC). He wanted to rouse Bennie, but Bennie was hard to rouse. The success of his last two books he owed, Junie pressed on, to this detached view of American society, a perspective he did not have when he was living in the Village. Bennie smiled. The fastidious Waterman said, "I've never thought of depriving one of my poor wretches of a front tooth."

Lutécie asked Fanny, "Have you read *Fair Is Foul?*"

"Yes I have. I thought it was just very *fine* . . ."

"*He* hasn't read *Fair Is Foul*," Lutécie declared on behalf of Bennie Jones. Bennie agreed. Lutécie said, in reference to the book's central relationship, "I must say, Junie, you'll forgive me, but that girl of yours mounts a very poor show." She stopped to laugh as she caught her own phrase returning, and then she continued, "I mean about *life* and *love*, she has no *artistic vision*. She seems to think dirty linens will serve as well as wine and roses. You've got them holing up like Sonya and Raskolnikov and they can't carry it off."

"I think of her as laid-back," said Junie, smiling, unruffled, content to have anybody reminded of Dostoevski. He was standing up, his left arm raised in a fascist salute, while Maryann with her tape measured him from armpit to hip. It was currently the style to wear ill-fitting home-made-looking sweaters, for which she had a natural talent. She was known as the Mad Knitter.

"I see a definite family resemblance, I really do," Maryann said, a kindly eye darting from tape to Fanny. In the lining up of forces for and against leaving Albi, she was pro-Carrie, one of the few. From the time she arrived in Albi twelve years ago she was ready to go back.

"No resemblance whatsoever," said Junie, sounding rude.

"Not the coloring, you know, but the same height, the same frame, the broad brow," Maryann continued, kind and friendly.

Twelve

CAROLINE Honora Foote did not take an entirely out-landish turn when she headed off abruptly with Lutécie Tavernier to an unheard-of section of France, the opinion of friends and the people on B Street notwithstanding. Her paternal grandmother came from this Provençal stock, and although dying at a great age while Carrie was still very young, only seven, she left her mark on the child's mind twice in the last year of her life. On her final Christmas the old grandmother came out of the closet with the Protestant Bible for her, French edition. It bore the wobbly inscription "To my granddaughter, December 25, 1938, John 3:16," a child who had never held a Bible in her hand. The impeccably free-thinking family took this defection with the compassionate understanding natural to liberals, noting her dotage, but did not translate John 3:16. It was many years too late when Carrie read, "For God so loved the world that he gave his only begotten Son, that whosoever believeth in him should not perish, but have eternal life."

More riveting and indeed consequential to Carrie was the old grandmother's dying after many months in a bed made up in the dining room where she had been brought so they could take care of her. At the end she didn't speak a word of English. She talked in a language not a soul knew, Occitan, the language of Provence. Her children could string together a little French but could not comfort her in what was her childhood tongue. It was a disturbing phenomenon.

This death occurred at a time when the goal of immigrants, and more particularly their children and grandchildren, was to be entirely American, not ethnic, altogether melted in the pot, and indeed the grandchildren, Marcus and Carrie, had the name of Foote instead of Hasenfuss as a consequence of Boston's extremely patriotic anti-German fever during World War I. It was from fear of being thrashed. If they had traced their lineage on either the German or the French side, they would quickly have run into peasants. Nonetheless, as products of the public schools the children thought of themselves as Americans to the marrow, direct descendants of the Founding Fathers and the *Mayflower*, all the way back to the blue-painted Picts. This early-rooted fiction is rarely superseded by known facts, and in the last few years Carric, although deriving in part from Provence, and a mistress of the language, had increasingly felt herself displaced in France, and was feeling compelled to go home to America, where she belonged. She was suffering from love of country, a now curious affliction.

Buying fish in the open market on Saturdays in the cathedral square, Carrie almost passed for a true regional type. She was dark, held her head erect with the straight-backed carriage of older French women of whatever class, the young having converted to slouching, of whatever class; but she was tall, as Fanny was. The Foote women ran tall,

somewhat buxom, built to last, and the men a little squat—
trapu is the French word. Around the choir of the cathedral
of Albi there are life-size figures from the Old Testament in
painted stone, looking like solid French burghers, and
described as *trapu*. If all the members of the Foote family
stood in a row and a board were put across their heads it
would lie flat. As to width, Carrie had spent her whole
adult life on a diet, had lost hundreds of pounds, the same
five over and over again, she thought. On the other hand at
nearly fifty she did not look gaunt and drawn, and the more
people liked her, the more handsome they found her.

Even those people who did not find Carrie handsome
regarded her as a great curiosity. She ran the Printing
House with panache but without any sort of democratic
discussion about the desuete and arbitrary rules she
imposed. In fact she didn't know she imposed any. She
didn't think tidying up for dinner was a rule. She'd been
out of touch for years. When Candace had sent Fanny off
to do her story, she assured her that a place like the Printing
House was a warren of conspiracies and passions and love
affairs of the swinging variety, that that's what those places
bred. But Carrie managed, at the price of God knows how
much personal agony experienced by the residents, to keep
what swinging there was a private affair.

Carrie was not insouciant, not philosophically an Imma-
terialist (Bishop Berkeley muttered darkly/If I can't see
you, you can't be you). All she expected was that none of
the swinging should come to public attention. The priority
for people who were there was their work, and whatever
each of them did in privacy, no matter how ingenious the
twist or how baffling, was of no moment, so long as he or
she didn't insist on leaving clues.

Whoever left Candace with the clue that Foote and Tavernier were the quintessential lesbians did not give it to the residents of the Printing House. They wondered about Carrie—whom she had loved, whether she had loved—but they wondered heterosexually, a failure of the imagination. She had been off now with Berg the Filmmaker for several days, and the only disagreement was whether *he* was gay, not whether she was. They agreed that she was excessively upright, but since they profited they kept their mouths shut, in the usual self-serving way. For those who did not think she should return to the States it was Exhibit A. She would be eaten alive.

But Carrie's life had taken one dramatic and fortuitous turn and she wanted it now to take another. There had been three obstacles to her return and they went down like ninepins. Or to be accurate, two went down and she knew she could tumble the other, poor dear. About a year ago there came a letter from Will Costello saying that he was thinking he would wind up his affairs and sell the thread mill. The idea of buying that factory and refitting it put a light under her longing to go home. So the first obstacle was merely money. But of course there was lodged at the back of her mind the misbegotten business with her family. The old trespass and the outraged reaction had long since lost all their point for her as well as for Marcus, although actually while each of them forgot the original heat of passion each remembered himself as the transgressor. Each had waited to be forgiven and in the meanwhile had become absorbed in a new phase of his own life. The accidents of time and distance allowed the momentary upheaval to set. A phone call, the coming of Megan, and that obstacle was on the way down. There remained one other.

Lutécie knew she was the other. She dug in her heels but she saw she was destined to die in Boston. Not even New

York. And why should two women of such disparate natures, tastes, and gifts find it unthinkable to go their separate paths? Particularly why was Carrie bound to Lutécie? Lutécie, once translated to France, had not changed her ways, pitched in and done some of the hard work of converting a very ticky tacky hostel for traveling salesmen into their classy establishment. She never took up hard work. And in fact, although Lutécie had been known to bat about when she lived in New York, she stopped batting once in Albi, and set about designing a version of the cloistered life for herself, intending possibly, by creating a more static world, to suspend time. She took up serious reading, she did her needlework, rather capriciously she began to teach herself Greek (although or because Carrie didn't know Greek), continued to stand on her head for the circulation, supported l'Association de sauvegarde du Vieil-Alby, and did not fail to enjoy the rather outré fact that she was in Albi at all. It was Carrie who had done all the batting, but it was Lutécie's eye for design, her taste for food, that taught Carrie everything she knew.

And moreover, in the beginning, it was Lutécie who drew the sort of people to the Printing House who are always nervously anxious about running out of places to go. She called herself the pension's tutelary goddess. Carrie said she was more in the order of an indigenous saint, very common in the scattered villages of the region, what is called a saint "canonized by the voice of the people." There was a somewhat similar St Gent who also stood on his head, and even had the custom of sleeping on his head, his feet in the air. He was buried upside down, and was known to get rid of persistent fevers. If you had a fever and you walked on your hands around his tomb you got a miraculous cure. At one time he was able to draw as many as twenty thousand pilgrims. The live Lutécie was not of course in that league, and they only needed thirty-five in residence, ten transient, to do well, but those she lured, in addition to word-of-mouth. The question was whether Lutécie could pull this trick in America, unaccustomed as it was to saints.

Lutécie did not want to pull this trick in America.

Although Carrie supported herself by innkeeping, she kept her hand in a cottage industry, reviewing history for historical journals, French and English. She had also been writing *The Life and Thoughts of a Single Woman*, for about a dozen years, the very dozen that had seen the rebirth of the women's movement. It was a still slim manuscript from her habit of throwing out a lot of observations—and in that resembled Fanny's master list. Also unlike Lutécie, who was a centripetal force, pulling people in, Carrie answered to the opposite, was impelled outward, frequently was off on little excursions, for the most part in rural France and northern Italy, but periodically she headed for the big city, London or Paris (although never New York or Boston. She'd never gone home). Sometimes people came along, the enthusiastic Titus taking her up on every invitation. And it was his father she had joined in London whenever he was on his way to Oxford. In fact, a lot of B Street turned up from time to time, one Reddish or another always arriving. They kept her up-to-date about Marcus and Elizabeth, Megan and the boys. Megan above all. She had loved that child. She hated losing her. In the end, that had been the worst wrench.

In the beginning the worst had been the renunciation of a passionate love, and Lutécie, who had spent her whole previous life in that field, was given to murmuring nervously that Carrie had given up too much, that perhaps she ought to reconsider, and so on. But Carrie said grimly, "You know what I'm giving up? I'm giving up, absolutely certainly, a life of tacking and trimming and fawning in the department, and in private, bobbing at the edges of somebody else's life." She had a natural bent for comparative history and in the years that followed she would look back at that renunciation, seeing it more in the nature of a cowardly flight, and thank her stars for her lack of courage. If she hadn't flown, she would not have left teaching, would not have Lutécie, the Printing House, the whole of France, wouldn't have had anything. "After all, Lu, you're the first to say that you can't measure the quality of your life by its sexual pleasure," she was able to add loftily a couple of years later when she was free of the obsession.

That Megan had become an unknown person was a distraction. From the moment of Marcus's call, Carrie's concentration was disturbed, and she put off work on a review of a book on Beowulf and the rise of capitalism, and went off with Berg, who was looking for a smaller town in a better-color red in which to film his very sordid *crime passionel*. First they drove up to Collanges, which he dismissed in a minute as unworthy of his subtle eye, and then they crossed the massif centrale into Provence to Rousillon, a town sitting on hills made of ochre of which there were seventeen shades, yellow through red, and which was happily able to satisfy Berg's sensibility. Now he had to steep himself, plunge in, breathe it all, and he put on a jogging costume, filled a knapsack with bread and cheese, took up an ash-plant stick brought along for the purpose, and said it would take him three days. Carrie took his car and drove to Cannes.

Thirteen

CARRIE returned to Cannes in grand style, in Berg's fancy BMW, which cost forty-five American dollars to fill up, and although to this day of a cheese-paring nature, headed for the Hotel Carleton, still five stars. She had first come to Cannes a young, poorish, diffident, self-effacing, scholarly woman in a worn but good-quality camel's-hair coat, and it was on one January morning in 1966, sitting in the winter sun, that she shed the lot. That is she had changed her coat immediately but it was from that day that she began to think it was possible to change the direction of her life. There and then she found herself determined to overthrow the determinism in things, throw her own shoe into her own machine.

She had come down to the French Riviera in January when it was only half as cold as it was in Boston, half as expensive as it was in April, and the hotels a quarter filled. Still, in winter, the promenade along the beach as well as the shop side of the boulevard de la Croisette is always crowded with elderly strollers. Aging women in fur coats and in great numbers carry their little dogs in their arms while their pale muffled husbands are maintained a half pace forward by an invisible leash. When the dogs indicate they are ready to relieve themselves, they are let down right in the middle of the sidewalk, while the husbands, drawn to a halt, pretending insouciance, stare out at the Mediterranean. French dogs have long had a certain presence.

At Cannes there is a crescent bay and a wide half circle of fine hotels facing the sunny sea and protected from the worst winter winds by the hills that rise immediately behind them to the Alps. The original old town is at the west end on a little hill of its own, and at the top of four flights of stone steps in a cul de sac there was a modest pension in which Carrie had settled for a week in a spare underheated room. She could see the sunshine on the water from her window. One morning, in a nervous but enterprising spirit, she had headed down the steps, crossed along the boat basin, passed flower beds filled with red cyclamen—known to her previously as a greenhouse plant in a Mother's Day pot—and when she reached the Hotel Carleton, she sucked in her cheeks and collar up, eyes half-lidded, walked through its doors, through its public rooms, to the bar. There she had let herself out onto a terrace protected by hedges in tubs, where there were tables and chairs all bathed in the lovely sun. Nobody had spotted her for an interloper, nobody stopped her. She had chosen her seat, settled in with her newspaper, and opened her coat.

Carrie was then thirty-four, with short brown hair which she was letting grow. She was pleasant-looking. She would tell Fanny that she thought of herself at that time as a person without physically distinguishing characteristics particularly since she had good teeth and there was not even a dental record in case her body was found in a wreck. (*"Exactly* how *I* feel!" Fanny would say.) There were to be many parallels of that sort. It is a psychological observation that a boy often resembles his uncle (sometimes to his father's chagrin) and in this era of feminism it is only fair that nieces may be discovered to take after their aunts. From girlhood Carrie would have liked to make a subtle but profound impression just by walking into a room, as from girlhood Fanny would have liked it. Fanny, however, was stalled at the threshold, everybody waiting for her to move, but in Carrie's day the fashion had been to push blindly on.

Carrie had pursued a scholarly career in French literature, and while earning her doctorate found her interests sidling off into Provençal, the language of her grandmother. Almost nobody else's interests sidled towards this subject, which was in one way good since she would not have to scratch her way through a thicket of scholars, but on the other hand her work was not destined to set the Rhône on fire. In July of 1965, with a semester's leave, some money saved from teaching, and a meager grant, she went off for six months to Avignon. She had begun her sojourn in high excitement, accompanied by the life and works of Frédéric Mistral, but could not sustain the pitch and finally fled to Cannes to end her stay in the last place that could be said to capture the homely spirit of this most famous of nineteenth-century Provençal poets. It was in Cannes that she put her life in review, mulling in her cul de sac over her subject, and over her affinity for culs de sac.

She'd been sitting on the Carleton terrace for about an hour amongst a dozen scattered guests when she heard the scraping of a chair behind her, and the cultivated American voice of a woman say, "The problem with the yacht, Bennie, is there's absolutely no privacy. If I have to be *at sea* I'd rather drift in a canoe with some cushions and a book."

"Told this fella be there by eleven. Got to straighten out

this radar contraption . . ." said a male American voice
with a touch of Down East drawl, as if party to another
conversation.

"Men who own yachts are awfully vulnerable. They
attract a disproportionate number of perfectly paltry people. Again and again I've been amazed at the *composure* with
which they bore you to death. *You* don't see them. You
don't talk to them, you're so busy running the thing, but *I*
. . . and what I don't like is reading in my cabin. I get cabin
fever and I *particularly* . . ."

"Thought we'd drive up to Vence for lunch. You like
that rack of lamb . . ."

". . . do not want to be stranded for four hours with
Arabella and Louie . . ."

"One-thirty"

"Let alone four *days*."

The man, Bennie, had left his position in the dialogue
and shambled off across the terrace and towards the yacht
basin. Very tall, lean, about sixty, he wore a windbreaker,
canvas deck shoes, and a sailor's cap with a visor.

Carrie had made plans to get a look at the woman in back
of her in an inconspicuous manner. It was the first American voice she had heard in weeks, the only one in Cannes.
Americans go to their own much warmer South in winter.
Cannes isn't really chic until the end of March.

At the time, Carrie would tell Fanny, she was on several
scores feeling impoverished and nursed her pride by
regarding the whole Côte d'Azur as beneath serious
thought, but even in the trough of her protective contempt
she had not ventured so far as to imagine that being sen-
tenced to four days on a yacht was really tough sailing. She
was delighted to hear it. She had walked along the moorings of the hundreds of boats resting in their winter berths

and had not wished for a passionate experience on one of them, but she had wished for a passionate experience per se. Something elegant, intellectual, sensual, but with a high moral tone. The fact that yachts were out was information she would pass on to Fanny. When finally she had turned in her seat as if searching for the waiter, the woman had gone.

The next morning Carrie had returned to the terrace with a sense of belonging, since she hadn't been thrown out the day before. But the American woman did not come and, Carrie thought, might very well have already been shanghaied. She took what had been the woman's seat, as she did again on the third morning, while bobbing a friendly nod to the waiter, and even called for an espresso. A number of sunning guests were now familiar, old husbands and wives, husbands and old mistresses, everybody unthreatening.

And then suddenly there was a shadow and the woman of the American voice said to Carrie, "I wonder if you will forgive me but if I could sit in the chair you're in I wouldn't get red pouches under my eyes. I've calculated the rays to a nicety. It's a problem that turns up at fifty. There've been a whole new set of problems. It's been quite a surprise."

As she had said, she wondered. And she had a look of query, her brows raised, a half smile, on a very beautiful fair face, set off by a kind of cloud of hair of the color that used to be called Titian. And green eyes. Impossible to think of fifty years. Carrie had said, "Why, I'd be *more* than happy . . ." and was on her feet on the instant, gathering her newspaper, book, bag not too gracefully, when the waiter brought her coffee.

"Oh *grand* you're American. I *crave* to talk American. I

thought you might be English but I hadn't looked at your shoes. May I take my coffee with you? Would you mind?"

"I would enjoy it," said Carrie, who had only minded being pegged so easily, and she had a little feeling of deflation, very familiar. "These were the days before international style," she would tell Fanny. "They were also the days when the Queen Mother, particularly in her hat, exemplified the British flair for clothes. That London was about to pop out with Carnaby Street and become the world's fashion leader would have been at that time beyond reasonable belief. I took the seat with my back to the sun."

They had ordered another coffee and Carrie had asked the woman where she was from. She thought most people tended to come from the Boston-Cambridge area.

"New York," said the woman, in the tone of a person who assumed, more statistically, that most people came from New York. "I was brought up in *Brooklyn*, actually, a great advantage. It gives you a sense of direction. Out. Makes you very *upward mobile*. But I was *born* in Toulouse, and do you know, as much time as I've spent over here I've never trotted back to give it a look?"

"Well, alas, they probably won't put up a plaque, then," said Carrie smiling, and added, "I had a grandmother who came from that region when she was a girl, but I don't know exactly where. What brought your family from Toulouse to Brooklyn? It's not a very usual migration, is it?"

"No, that's right. My father was a violist, a very *good* violist and played in the symphony of Toulouse, but he had a large family, I was the youngest, and he got the opportunity through some connections to join the Metropolitan Opera Orchestra in New York. He thought he could improve his situation. And he was put onto some other people from Toulouse who'd gone over and settled in a little neighborhood, a part of Brooklyn called Cypress Hills, where the cemeteries are, where half New York buries itself—our backyard. My mother still lives there. By herself. Rents the downstairs . . . She's a very independent eighty-one—and would love to come back for a visit, but I've never managed to . . . it's been on my conscience. On my conscience for *thirty years*," she said, with the musing half smile of regret that her conscience should be disturbed by anything, or so it seemed, because then she added, "By and large I'm not one to worry about my sins of omission."

Carrie laughed. "I have such an overactive conscience I could rent out space. I could take your mother on and leave you quite free."

"Ah, but you can tell that you have *character*. It's written on your face. I thought immediately I saw you that you'd strayed by error into this rather decadent habitat. What are you doing here?"

Carrie, uneasy about poaching on five-star territory and also about her fine character, had felt impelled to tarnish this. "On the contrary, I've strayed deliberately, came down here looking for a little debauchery, something mildly lurid, but in vain," she said darting a look of meaning at the elderly guests. "What I've been doing for the last five or so months is gathering material for a book on the Provençal— the language, the poet Mistral. I've been staying in Avignon but it's bloody cold there, and well, in the end I headed towards the sun for a week. I fly back to Boston on Saturday."

"And how does the book go?"

"Well, that's the strangest thing," said Carrie, who was subject to confessional impulses, a Foote trait that would be running strong in Fanny, too. "The book is going to plan, but increasingly I've begun to think my focus is too . . .

timid, too *obedient* . . . and that I was capable of a much vaster comprehension, that my scope could be much larger. It may be just an attack of grandiosity. It feels as though I'm gathering clouds into my arms. Of course, there's always the problem in my field, in any field, I suppose, of where you are in the spectrum—of knowing too much about too little, or too little about too much. And I, I don't know . . . I am suddenly ravenous to know a lot about a lot. Anyway, I'm wondering if I have the courage to throw up what I've done on this book . . . It's a little like having a child and then after a few years saying, 'I don't really like being the mother . . . ' " Carrie had said this, offering what was a bizarre analogy in those days.

"No, *no*, I don't think that's it at all," said the woman in a rush of support. "I was *haunted* when I was a girl with something *very like*. When I was eighteen I ran away to marry, and it wasn't much after that—not a *year*—when I thought, My God, this whole long life ahead of me, and I'm to sleep with only *one man!* I was shaken to the roots."

Carrie had blinked uncertainly and then laughed again. She had not slept with even one man and meant to sit on this fact. "Well," she asked, "and did you . . . work it out?"

"My God, yes. Over and over again. But the truth is when it isn't your problem any more, it doesn't seem very interesting. *Now*, I'm becoming simply obsessed with making provision for my *declining years*, and you know, I'm not at all taken with the suggestion of spending them in bed. You're young, and in fact your best years are ahead. The *best years* for a woman are the decade that begins at the end of the thirties," she said with an authority to which she looked entitled.

"That's very cheering, I must say," said Carrie, feeling

as though she were listening to good news from the tea leaves.

"You're not married?" the ringless Carrie was asked.

"No," said Carrie, to the woman whose fingers were covered with rings, possibly like military medals, one for each engagement. "I've loved men . . . up to a point. And I have been wistful to find a lifelong companionship but I've never been . . . deeply, passionately enough in love to . . ."

"Oh, well, they don't go together, that's why."

"So I understand. Still . . ." Carrie, flustered, had come to a fork in her thoughts with the two paths blocked. She was about to say that she had been drawn to people who were not available, who were married, but she thought it would make her sound like a Bobbsey Twin. She was then going to take refuge in her conviction that she had been committed to her work, without which a life had little meaning, but that seemed precious, especially to a woman who probably never had known a day's work.

"And you have your *work*," said the woman surprisingly and with firmness. "You may have a *crise de confiance now*, but all the higher to rise! You've put all those layers down. I take a very geological point of view. It's like peat or like compost or there's something there to mine. You're *essentially* substantial. But *I'm* all veneer, and I worry about my *Times* obituary. I wouldn't mind if it said 'She was a scandal and the mistress of three famous men,' in the spirit of Alma Mahler. I wouldn't balk . . . but I'm afraid they will clean it up and call me Prominent New York Hostess. I find it degrading, so much so that bone lazy though I am, I've been casting about to write a new script for myself for cover, like a palimpsest, I think it's called."

Carrie, who had been of course instantly curious to know

what her name was and who were the three famous men, had forborne and asked instead, "Do you have inclinations toward any . . ."

"Only negative ones. I don't want to marry. I don't want to spend my twilight years on a yacht. What I'd really like actually is my own *cell*, with a single bed and bare white walls—white is always better. I go wrong when I move into colors. I think, as a matter of fact, that you can do some very interesting things with cells." She was smiling, amusing herself. She went on, "There used to be provision for women of my age, the great religious houses, with quite good service, good food, one's own spiritual director . . . Well, I don't want a *spiritual* director—someone *bookish*. I need the right books. I've got to the point where I only want to know things that are *worth knowing*. Whatever I'm reading, I always think I ought to be reading something else . . . Ah, here you're back, Bennie. I've just found an American. We're talking about *maiden beds!*" And turning to Carrie she said, "I am Lutécie Tavernier and this is my friend Benedict Jones."

"My name is Caroline Foote," said Carrie, disappointed not to recognize either name and in another moment couldn't remember what they were.

The man shook her hand courteously, sat down, ordered Bloody Marys for them "because it's proper to raise glasses when good countrymen get together," and said to Carrie, "Glad Lu's found you. She's always looking for a better class of people. Yup. True." He grinned and looked off. He had a weathered lined New England face and a confident slouch.

"You're damn right. She's a *scholar*. I've got culture shock after all those Blue-Footed Boobies . . ."

The man was pleased that Carrie was a historian. He himself had a bent that way he said. He had been interested to discover that this section of the Mediterranean coast wasn't developed until the last century. The area was outside the law, the province of pirates, terrorized by Saracens. He had been tracking the routes the Saracens followed.

"He's got a yacht for his old age. He wants to set up tours, be a historical-tour director," said Lu.

"The Saracens were what all pirates around here were called right through the nineteenth century. They controlled the coast until 1840, when the English aristocracy moved in," said Bennie.

"Now it's been captured by the arts and crafts," said Lu.

"Caves, coves, hideouts. Very interesting to map out."

"It's an improvement scheme. Everybody who goes on his tour gets a reading list," said the woman to Carrie, and then to Bennie she said, "It will be a real breakthrough for Arabella. Her first book."

"All the shipping hugged the shore, so that the sailors could swim to safety if the boat sank. They sank in enormous numbers."

"I don't think Arabella can swim a lot better than she can read."

They invited Carrie to join them for lunch in Vence at the Auberge des Seigneurs, and when she looked uneasy, they assured her the food was very nice. She demurred saying she wasn't dressed . . .

"The coat! You're just right for the coat! It needs the right neck. You must try it. You don't have to take it if you don't like it, but I feel the collar's too wrong for me. My head settles in like Napoleon's. I hate to live with my own mistakes. Well, I see I've embarrassed you. We'll go to lunch, and then after you can decide . . . you'll know us better."

They drove, three in the front seat, of a Bentley, a car Carrie had never been in before, and it was safe to say, would never be in again. The restaurant was a Simple Inn. The food was the best she had ever eaten in her life, the wine the best she had ever drunk, and while deliriously happy, she did not get to know either the woman or the man at all better. Nonetheless when they got back to Cannes, she went up to see the coat, took it, and was kissed good-bye. Beyond their being Lu and Bennie, she would tell Fanny, she never learned their names.

Fourteen

For some weeks there had frequently been a BMW parked half on the sidewalk in front of the Printing House. It had a bumper sticker which read FOAT WUTH AH LUV YEW, and the French-speaking people thought it must be a slogan in Occitan. The Provençal did not. Fanny was coming back at noon on Wednesday when she noted the car, noted the sticker, but did not expect to understand it. She was trying to take in the experience of the bishop's palace, where she had spent the morning and where she had not been twenty minutes when she was asking herself, What kind of a world is this if I didn't even know these pictures existed, this museum existed! Unexpectedly at her elbow, there was Titus to provide the answers. He had rushed through some work so that he could introduce her to the Lautrecs, he said, because some of the portraits have interesting regional associations. He wondered if she'd read Proust, and when she said No, he said there was of course the inevitable association of Lautrec's Paris paintings with Proust's *maisons de passe*. He then advised her to wait until her French was good enough so as not to read him in translation. She would have liked to say to him, "You know what my inevitable association is? What my mother says about your father, that he marches in on every subject tending to sound like the Boy Jesus Astonishing the Elders!" But she merely gave him her strained attention.

He said, "Alain thinks you look like *l'Anglaise*. Come on, I'll show you," and he drew her along, skipping several rooms, which she really despised doing, and brought her in front of a portrait of a childish, unintelligent, not at all good-looking frowsy music-hall "star."

"I look like that?" she yipped, now quite frantically exasperated and also mortified.

"I don't think you look at all like that. You have a very strong face. It's your hair. He sees your hair. He hasn't really got a subtle eye. You know who has hair like yours? Gina Reddish has hair like yours. She's very attractive." Titus thought he was implying that Fanny might take the compliment by extension.

In the matter of her appearance Fanny's hair was a sore point, one of seven. Gina was also a sore point. The very thought of her had the mysterious instant effect of greatly enhancing the value of TX. She suddenly pined for TX. She looked at *l'Anglaise*, insipid, confident, happy, sly, and saw her as everything she was not.

"She's *something*," she said out loud, intending a double entendre, a rebuke, a withering rebuke to herself. "I'm going back to the beginning," she added. "I really don't like to skip around." She left.

Titus was aware that he'd put Fanny off. He was helplessly clumsy about women, he thought. Alain hadn't been here two months and had already had two American girl friends, or what passed for girl friends—he and Gina had gone off for a couple of days. Titus had looked on coolly amused, urbane. In fact women scared him to death. Sexually he was yearning, romantic, capable of the most dashing and outrageous acts of love imaginable (what now pass for routine). But what he really needed was a woman who liked a snail's pace, who was driven wild by unsureness, hesitancy. He would like to "lay her in lillies and in violets." He was into all that. But he was born too late, and he kept getting older. And he stayed on at the Printing House dawdling. Ironically he could look at *l'Anglaise* with something like recognition. He had been a client in one of these establishments in Brussels. He gave it up in fright and in the nick of time. He had exactly the kind of sentimentalizing nature which made him fall in love with one of these women, try to rescue her. The trouble lay in an inability to separate love and sex. He sighed, shoved his hands in his trouser pockets, hunched his shoulders, and wheeled around to look for Fanny. He found her in a brown study, sitting on a camp chair vacated by a guard.

"Listen," he said in a reassuring tone, "don't worry about the Proust. When I came here my speaking French was terrible and what I used to do is I'd drop in at l'Eglise de Saint-Salvi for mass, two or three times a day. It's in the vernacular now, of course, and the priest speaks very clearly, and you get to hear the cadences, your ear catches it. It's better than the tube because it's repetitious, you see. I'll tell you something funny. I thought I'd just about gotten hold of it, maybe my *last mass*—and the priest came up to me. He recognized me by this time you know. He reached out for my hand and he said, "My son, you appear to be having some trouble?' And I shook hands and said, 'Not any more father, thank you. I'm all right now.' So then we parted quite happy with what we seemed to have done for each other."

"I think that's a very nice story," Fanny said, smiling, and he thought she was feeling friendly towards him again. She too was in a restored mood when she left him to go back to the pension, thinking that after all it had only been five days, not five years as it felt, since she'd seen TX and she might just casually drop him an amusing postcard. She passed the BMW with its sticker and, now a familiar, went around by the back pantry door and let herself in through the kitchen. There, lying on the kitchen table, laid out on butcher's paper, were four long skinned bodies, each with the head of a rabbit, and four furry paws. On a chair sat a basket of Golden Delicious apples. Surveying the apples and the rabbits, side by side, were Mme Maury and Carrie, both with their arms akimbo, in a state of war. Carrie looked up at this strange intruding person uncertainly, her mind on rabbit recipes, and didn't recognize her niece. Wild horses couldn't have dragged from Mme Maury the news of her arrival.

Fanny, surprised as well, said hesitantly, "Carrie?"

That shy sound, and the now entirely recognizable smile went right to Carrie's heart, and she was around the table, her arms around Fanny in a second. "Megan, Megan, Megan," she said, actually finding herself crying. As quickly, Fanny was crying. Mme Maury, stony, did not cry.

"Oh, what a *beautiful* girl you are. Your eyes are so *wide apart*. The *same eyes*. Why I didn't see it immediately? It's that Mme Defarge. She is *so* exasperating. She's pestered me for rabbit for ages, and then I found them at a good price and brought them back and she won't touch them with the paws still on. She says it's unlucky. Oh, the *heads*, the *heads*, she'll chop those off with pleasure, she's as mean . . . and she knows it's the law. They've got to keep the

head and paws on to prove they aren't selling you a cat."
They were both now done crying, and were laughing. Not
Mme Maury.

"I thought a rabbit's foot was *good* luck," said Fanny.

"Not attached! Oh Megan, Megan, let's get out of here."
And Carrie turned to Mme Maury and said in stern French,
"You will tell Marie-Laure that we will take our lunch alone
upstairs, *if* you please."

Once upstairs alone they began to talk ardently about
things neither had the least interest in—Maryann's knitting
worsted and what a number of wool shops there were in
Albi. Carrie talked although she wanted to listen, and by
listening have herself restored to the old normal belonging
to a fond family: even though there was nothing normal
about a fond family any more. Fanny was content with the
evidence of having been really missed, her photographs taking a lot of wall space above the writing desk, and to be
looked at with such uncritical pleasure, always a winning
point of view. Carrie did not, however, like the changing of
her name, and did not know whether she could manage it.
Carrie's two rooms were banked with her belongings, books
and pictures running up to the ceiling, the furniture hud-
dled on two island rugs, one in the middle with a sofa and
chairs, the other around a table by the French windows
looking out into the chestnut leaves.

"I love all this," said Fanny, moved by the mellow look
of things in their resting place. She thought she could mem-
orize the color tones and copy them.

"When I was young," said Carrie, "I believed the best
policy was not to allow yourself to become encumbered
with *things*, so that if anything good turned up, you could
go off like a shot. And, indeed, so it happened. Something
good did turn up and off I went. But in Albi I discovered

that while part of my nature was Spartan, another part was in fact quite acquisitive, and I resolved this duality by making everything fit into two rooms. I understand that the mark of an amateur philosopher is that he divides everything in two. I divide all of life in two: into a private life and a public life. There's usually quite a discrepancy." She laughed and then referring to her things she said, "Oh, if I could sell the lot. But it's not worth much. I'd really like to get a hold of some money." She was taking china from a cupboard, and setting silver on the table as she talked. The meal was brought in, she poured the wine, and she said, "Lutécie's rooms are almost spare. I don't know whether you've been in them? No, well the thing is that everything she's got is the genuine article, no exposition posters, nothing like that. It's really quite annoying what a difference there is. When I come back here my overstuffed chairs look like water buffaloes at a water hole."

Fanny laughed, protested, murmured, drank her wine, ate her omelet, cheese, and bread, peeled an apple (*un goldén*), marveled how it all looked and tasted entirely French and in essence altogether different from the exact noon meal served every day in Boston and New York, the same she had herself served. And Carrie looked French to her somehow, a racy Victorian French, sitting with a straight back, her dark dyed hair piled on her head, a black sweater over a yellow-printed blouse, a little overstuffed like her chairs, but still with style. She had a lot of French style, which Fanny examined.

"Well, now tell me, how did this all come about? What was it *finally* brought you here?" Carrie asked unexpectedly. She found herself greatly relieved by Megan. She had been nervous about another Gina Reddish.

"What brought me here?" Fanny repeated, smiling

uncomfortably. She'd slipped away from waiting to be asked. "*False pretenses* brought me here. I work for people who want to do a story on the Printing House, and they'll stop at nothing. I've been there, at *First*, for three years, where *I* learned how to stop at nothing."

"Oh that's What's-her-name? She's been after us for ages," said Carrie impatiently. "I can't *imagine* what she thinks is going on here!"

"She thinks, of course, that you're the quintessential *feminists*, sort of *vintage*, you know. And I agreed to try for entirely selfish reasons. It was a squirrel cage there. And there are *no jobs*. So it was a tremendous break, when she discovered who I was, who *you* were . . . I'd never been to Europe. And actually, Carrie, from the moment you left I had every intention of finding you again, so I thought, the Lord uses mysterious means. My father says he'll buy me out. I haven't the least compunction, taking his money now. I've absolutely loathed this dopey family feud, and now it seems there was *never* sufficient reason. My father's so vague and my mother says it was only because you were in . . . Of course if I were to do the article, you would certainly have the final . . ."

"What did your mother say?"

"What?"

"What did your mother say about my leaving?"

"She said . . . that you were in love with . . . a married man."

"Who does she say it was?"

Fanny, very uneasy, straightened the knife and fork on her plate.

"Who was it?" Carrie asked again, mildly, and not angry in any way.

"Mr. Sidney. David Sidney," Fanny watched to see how

that went. Carrie had a quite delighted look on her face.

"It's so curious what people make of one's life, how they fill in the gaps, isn't it?"

"I remember one day, we were in Rockport and you confided in me that . . . you were in love. You looked so happy . . ."

"Oh, I remember that day. You kept throwing your bread into the wind and it would fly back in your face. One person I always loved was *you*."

Fanny waited for something more but Carrie was not forthcoming. They talked about the family and Carrie's toying with the possibility of returning to B Street. She then went on to say that Fanny ought not to be too hard on *First,* and that women of every shape and age got courage from the movement to take charge of their own lives, and that Fanny might give the article a try.

Fifteen

Fanny's introduction into the Printing House affected its ecology the way people of much richer substance did not. Junie Waterman's publisher had arrived, an expansive man able to predict what would be the specific economic and moral calamities consequent upon there being a Republican administration, the sort of informed opinion expatriates, in this instance every one a gloomy Democrat, took very literally. The publisher had a short, participatory wife, ardent, there to correct his details, and described by Titus as the kind of person you sit next to at a dinner party and find yourself solemnly promising to read the complete works of a poet you never heard of.

In the south wing meanwhile, where the people in music were generally contained, the preliminary arrangements for a new production of *Der Rosenkavalier* were coming to a crescendo, echoing through the ventilating shafts, reverberating everywhere, and stimulating Lutécie to a burst of song on her own part, and a lot of searching the memory for musical phrases. She was prepared to translate with gestures for whoever was about; for Fanny—" 'My dear Hip-

polyte, today you've made me into an old woman.' You
don't know it? That's what the beautiful Marschallin says
to her hairdresser. It's very sad. I sang it *one whole year*.
Carrie will tell you." Then another piece of lyric, measured
for Fanny, and translated pointedly, "It's always one wet
eye and one dry eye." Her voice was still pleasant.

Fanny was by accident a catalytic factor at the pension.
She was certainly a friendly warm young woman, but it
was as though the temperature at the Printing House had
been stuck at 31°F. and needed only to rise a crucial two or
three degrees. She was unaware that by her presence, by
inadvertence, other people had been made quite anxious.
She herself was anxious, and also disoriented. For one
thing, in the week that followed her coming, she was regu-
larly surprised at what time it was. Twice a day she found
herself with a terrific appetite, hurrying back along the rue
de la Temporalité, thinking appositely, about time, about
how the hours of the day accomplished more in France than
they did at home, about how much more thought was
required to manage them, as it seemed.

She had been poking about the town, as well as the pension, getting the pulse of the place for her article, and found
the beat strong, steady, everyone full of regular habits,
accomplishing things from one end of the day to the other.
She never would have credited such a hive of inner-
directed, undeflected workers as was that Printing House,
every morning everybody racing to his typewriter, racing
to his violin. To have a sense of vocation was to Fanny the
most wished-for and unattainable of blessings. She had a
true vocation for mind drifting. Once in college she had
tried out an introductory lecture to a course on understanding music. The first rule was not to allow one's thought to
wander, and she left on that discouraging note. Did she

want to be a writer? She had lately picked up Rilke's *Letters to a Young Poet* and read that the first test of a true writer was the compulsion to write night and day. Another F. About the Printing House she thought it was just possible that what kept everybody productive and orderly might be the food. The wonderfully serious provision of two sessions of French cooking daily, the certainty that those hours, noon and evening, were bracketed for eating French food, drinking French wine, would be very mollifying when one's work was going badly, and well deserved when it wasn't. "I suppose," she had suggested, smiling encouragingly to her frequent companion the sociologist Alain, "if you asked what percentage of American expatriates decided to stay because of the food you'd get a hundred." He said nobody had ever given him that answer.

The next day, caught up in how oddly French time was passing, she said to Alain, "Don't you think it is strange that a street on church property would be called Temporality: *Eternity*, I would have thought."

"Is not odd. Is very common," Alain assured her, just as Titus hove into sight, but she would be damned if she would ask Titus why. The three went off together for a cappuccino and Alain proposed to Fanny that they borrow Carrie's car and drive down for the weekend to the Mediterranean coast, for instance to Narbonne, where they could still count on sunny weather at this time of the year. Titus, not included in this invitation, said that the beaches at Narbonne were man-made and might be the only ugly beaches in the entire world, if Fanny found that sort of thing interesting. Narbonne itself was another matter.

"Really nice small city on a canal, and the funny thing is that it was actually destined to have the third-largest Gothic cathedral in France . . ." Nobody's cool was more dis-

turbed by the warm Fanny than Titus's. Fervently he did
not want to see another American girl breeze off with
Alain.

"At this moment," said Alain, "Queen Elizabeth is on
the regal cruise in the Mediterranean with reliable weather.
Today's paper! Still, Titus is correct. Funny gray, the
beaches. Better to go on to the Carmague, you think?" This
to Titus.

"They built this tremendous *choir*, so enormous that it
hit smack into the ramparts of the city. There was no room
left for the nave. And that was it! They have one-half a
cathedral," persisted Titus. He and Alain had exchanged
some not very penetrating remarks on the subject of liberated women and what Titus called their new round heels.
Alain thought it was a very nice characteristic in the Americans. He had severe reservations in regard to French
women, causing Titus a twitch of patriotic annoyance.

Fanny declined Alain's invitation. She would be going
off on a little toot with Carrie, she said. Privately she
thought she could not have gotten an interesting conversation going, whether because of their language difficulties
she was not sure. She thought this really attractive man did
not really turn her on, and was reminded of that something
wanting in TX, another attractive man. Or the something
wanting was in her. It made her very worried. "And I've
got a lot of work to do on this article," she added.

Titus was relieved of the prospect of having to pass a
weekend sunk in ignominy had Fanny gone off. This was
not because Fanny was of singular interest to him. All
women were of singular interest to this compulsive girl
watcher. And actually he was angry at Fanny. She had
been found wanting in sensitivity. He was disappointed
that she meant to go ahead with the article, although his

reaction had nothing whatever to do with the fear of an exposé, that she would turn up and exploit some scandal. Not at all. It was his deep disdain for any sort of cheap popularizing, which he spotted all over the place, the way St. Dominic spotted the devil's hand. The tone of the Printing House, its social comedy, its aesthetic dimension, its moral seriousness, could not be conveyed in some vulgar mass-circulation sheet. And should not. In the course of time Carrie might offer her *Life and Thoughts of a Single Woman* for publication, and that would be the sum and substance. Titus had a gallant nature, was protective of Carrie and even half in love with her. However, he believed that while she might make a Colette, he was at best a failed Chéri. He was too old. He was thirty. Ten years ago, maybe, when he was in his Byronic period . . . Whatever woman of whatever condition, he was able to find himself disqualified.

On Friday when he was passing through the kitchen on his way to the Archives, Carrie said, "I was thinking that tomorrow I might take Megan down to Castres, or if it's nice maybe go on to the Château de Lastours, drive around that country. We could have lunch at Réalmont. You want to come along?" She was sitting at the table peeling and quartering apples. "I have a new recipe for *tarte Tatin*. It is fraught with dangers," she added, to give Titus time to say yes.

Titus was surprised by the invitation. "Can't do it, Carrie, I've got to get through this last incunable. It's been pulling teeth and I don't like to lose my momentum." And then breaking into his own solemnity, which he was always the first to do, he said, "Momentum. I call it momentum. It's lying on the floor with its feet up in the air but I call it momentum."

Carrie was eating an apple, looking thoughtful. "Don't you like her?" she asked. Her pleasure in the return of a solid authentic Megan, not prepackaged, was a public matter in the Printing House.

"Did you know that Byron couldn't bear to see a woman eat? Now I like to see a woman eat. I like the lusty look of it," he said, and he picked up an apple, settled into a chair, and hooked one arm around its back. "Since you mention her, I want to tell you that I don't think she should be encouraged to write that article. I think you ought to tell her to knock it off."

Carrie chewed her apple. Finally she said, "This is a big break for her. And after all, the Printing House . . . well, you know, the development of the capital letter right *here* would make a really interesting story. Mrs. Wilson would be glad . . ."

"You may find it hard to believe but they aren't probably interested in the history of movable type. The type they are interested in is you, and Lu, and Junie, and what they want to know about Junie is whether he sleeps with the transients. That's all. And they would be disappointed to hear the answer." Privately Titus took some comfort from Junie Waterman's presumed fidelity. One less man screwing around.

"Listen," he said, lounging against the kitchen table, waving a finger vaguely in the air, possibly conducting the recorded orchestral music that was filtering through the vent, "you and I have done a lot of quite frank talking, but it has not, of course, escaped my notice, you know, that we avoid such events as what culminated in your taking off with Lu all those years ago. Now I can tell you that what was called your *flight* had quite a remarkable impact on B. Street. My own unflappable father flapped. I was only a kid but it brought *me* up short. All right, all right, it's your business. But if Fanny's going to do an article, surely she's entitled to ask what precipitated all this . . ." Titus paused because there was Fanny, frowning, fixed in attention.

Fanny had been returning home through the pantryway when she had caught the words "B Street," and they brought her to a halt in the frame of the door. By some trick of the brain she didn't recognize Titus sideways, strung out as he was with his legs crossed. She saw instead an older man of composure, of easy authority, in the tailored English jacket, shirt, and tie that she always privately found very . . . evocative. In, of course, the next split second it was only Titus. Still she was left with the print on her mind of Carrie treating him, and Titus acting, like an equal. There was that elusive adult poise she did not have herself. Piqued by her own shortcomings she said in a huff, "Really Carrie, I'm ready to forget the whole damn thing. It's been so . . . *frantic*-making from start to finish . . . the silly feud . . . the mysterious allusions. Whatever the *culminating* circumstances, however you met Lutécie—well, I mean I just have trouble crediting that it's a case of *significant misprision.*"

"Good," said Titus. "Eloquent. I like eloquence. Now Carrie *thinks*," he continued, smiling broadly, "that your *First* editor will be much moved by the history of type design. Does she *know*, for instance, that Roman capital letters were meant to represent the noble proportions of the human body? And another *fascinating* story is the . . ."

"Oh, for heaven's sake, be quiet, Titus!" said Carrie, unhappy to have provoked Megan. "It's just a private matter, Megan. It isn't even interesting. Of course, I realize that privacy, discretion aren't the current admired values, that I'm hopelessly out of touch, despite everything Titus can do," she added, not wanting to provoke Titus either.

"I take her to all the Woody Allen movies I can," said Titus, who needed little encouragement in a conversation. "They're very big in Albi. And of course I fill her in on the latest in karma kickbacks, supply-side sex, macrobiotics—I *try* to keep her finger on the American pulse, but it always rises up to point a moral." He illustrated with his own finger, which was waving about anyway.

"I don't like Woody Allen movies," said Carrie, identifying a subject upon which she took a position.

"Actually Carrie likes *Casablanca*."

"One summer a few years ago, when was it? It was before you came, Titus. But Cordelia and Lucia were visiting, and Gina Reddish, and we had this quite vehement division of opinion, the girls and I, about *Casablanca* and one of the Woody Allen movies. It was quite generational. Alain would love to have taped us. They thought that Ingrid Bergman's renouncing her passion for Humphrey Bogart in order to stand by her husband would not be credible today. They thought about everybody they knew and didn't know a single person who would do that. I said, 'At the end of the movie didn't you feel there was something answered *larger* than *personal gratification?*' And Cordelia said yes and she also felt that way at the end of *Iphigenia at Aulis.*"

"Of course if your name is Cordelia you might be ambivalent about sacrifice," said Titus.

"I liked a couple of his movies," said Fanny, almost compulsive about admitting to some weakness or other.

"What do you suppose the Moral Majority makes of them?" Carrie asked sternly, and answered, "They see in his characters people with *no real handicaps*. They see life with no holds barred, quite *visibly* no holds barred, and that it doesn't work. They see people with all the sex they want, money to spare, professional success, and self-pity *galore*. Nobody is happy. Everybody forlorn and helpless. Plots without even the *suggestion* of an elusive moral excellence, and what I minded was the girls *falling* for the idea that people who listen to Mozart were really helpless in a corrupt materialist world . . ."

"You know, they say in *Australia* everything that is intellectual or refined is called *trendy*," said the irreverent Titus.

"Well, your sisters are far from helpless, and *Gina!*" Carrie continued, sitting erect, in full sail, seeming to draw her breath from the very air their brother Titus might have been planning to breathe. "They live in *America*. They're not at *risk* if they speak out, they're not exiled, flung into prison!"

"I'm not going to take her to another Woody Allen movie," said Titus.

"You're right of course, Megan—Fanny—it is not a matter of significant misprision, but Titus is right too. I don't see how you can do an article about the Printing House that would interest *First* . . . I don't see how it would look in a magazine like *First*."

" 'Shrined in a hog's turd,' " said Titus, borrowing from Chaucer.

Fanny, who had been standing, swung herself into a kitchen chair, laughing, noticing suddenly how relieved she was not only to be free of the article but of the grip *First* had had on her. She took an apple and ate it, thinking, not listening, while Carrie and Titus bantered on about other things.

Sixteen

As soon as it was understood that Fanny would not write her article, that she would lose her job and was plunged into debt, several people liked her better. She spent some of her now freed hours with Lutécie and the Watermans, often in concert. Lutécie, laid up, summoned her for company, and Junie befriended her for reasons of a new book, probing her for a young and representative psyche, throwing himself into his questions with terribly sincere tenderness, captivating Fanny. He liked Fanny. He wasn't exactly using her. And Fanny understood the terms, and did not at all mind being the interesting subject, or interesting object, of an established celebrity. He wanted to hear from a twenty-six-year-old woman and she was ready to sing.

Lutécie was more literally and a little cynically continuing her singing. "Thou shalt dash them in pieces like a potter's vessel!" was the refrain. She had switched from Strauss to Handel, felled by arthritic pain. Carrie had been trying to persuade her to change her regimen, at least to give up standing on her head, but she was adamant, until

Friday morning when she could not stay up there. On Saturday she could not easily move and a doctor was summoned. Carrie and Fanny called off their weekend excursion, and Alain was not there for a backup. Fanny was one American girl who had turned him down, but he had a spare, and off he had gone with the spare in the car, and that, for Fanny, was the end of Alain. The doctor said that Lutécie might have broken a rib or two, that God made people grow brittle with age, agreeing more or less with Handel. He thought she should go into the hospital for X rays and tests. She said Out of the Question. Carrie turned up the heat in Lutécie's rooms, a measure of her concern.

Lutécie's rooms were on the first floor and had very high ceilings to collect the heat. The walls were oyster white, the furniture small, spaced, no lumbering armoire. Fanny was properly awed by the number of handsome and disparate things—a Byzantine crucifix by the side of a Picasso bacchanal—that lived in peace and quiet with each other. There was evidence of fine needlework throughout the Printing House and Lutécie was the leading needleworker. Although kept to her room, she had propped herself in a chair before a large screen of stretched buckram. When Fanny came in she was talking to Junie and Maryann, working a needle back and forth very slowly, looking something like a harpist playing in a mournful symphony, her eyes darting back and forth to a picture nailed to the frame mast.

She explained to Fanny, "It's a detail of the *Creation of Adam*, the one in the Accademia di Belle Arti in Florence, just Adam and God. You must fix your eye on each thread. I'm on the feet. Now Adam's not really quite altogether finished, if you notice his feet, still feet of *clay*, still *unformed*, as opposed to the nicely delineated toes of God."

Lutécie and her work were necessarily very well lighted, her face a bit of a shock, lined and yellow like a withering apple, *un gol-dén*.

Fanny had been invited to Sunday lunch. The table was set on white linen. She thought not for the first time that half the people in Albi must be in the laundry business, but she said, "We had a Chardin exhibit at the Boston Museum of Fine Arts and every meal I've had since I've been in France reminds me of those pictures. We eat the same food and it never looks like a Chardin."

They had transferred Lutécie to the table with some difficulty, and were now settled, and Maryann asked, "Did you major in art, Fanny?"

"You can visit a museum without majoring in art," said Junie, unpleasantly. Junie was a bad-tempered faithful husband, of which there seem to be more than one might suppose. Carrie put it to resentment at leading an upright life while all around were horizontal. She thought it would have been a break for Maryann if he had strayed and had it on his conscience.

"I was wondering whether you majored in art because I notice how often you have visited the Lautrecs," said Maryann easily. She would not be baited, a constant challenge to Junie.

"Well, as a matter of fact, there was the most *curious* thing," said Fanny enthusiastically, and in an attempt to cover what she thought was the general embarrassment. "I mean usually there are only a few people in there. Of course it's not the tourist season. But this morning, well, there was a sort of enormous *herd* of elderly people, Golden Age peasants, do you think?"

"Marvelous!" said Junie.

"And they were being rather firmly hustled along by a

woman about my age with henna hair and tight pants, very Haute Punk, you know, and here was her group, all of them looking like Mme Maury, wearing that old black that turns brown, and she'd get them in front of a brothel scene, and rattle off what sounded like the most *sophisticated* spiel—which I couldn't understand. And they stood there, stone faced, like Mme Maury, not a quiver. You wonder what they must make of it. I saw a bus outside . . ."

"Terrific," said Junie. "I may have to use it."

"The girl was wearing jeans," said Fanny, who was wearing a skirt, "and the label was in English and it said 'Weavers, Jeanmakers since 1970.' I wrote it down."

"Great," said Junie. He seemed to gather in her observations like a croupier. He was delighted with her. And without, evidently, any memory of the earlier exchange with his wife, he said to her with kindly interest, "Did you major in English, Fanny? I think somebody said that you would like to write."

A bad question. Unlike the other people, Fanny did not find herself enhanced by suddenly having no job, no money, no future. She said, "I guess I don't really know what I want to do. I don't have a sense of vocation, true vocation. It's the worst sort of . . . because what I really fear is a *fragmented* life—episodic. Things seem to be set up that way now, sequential, moving from person to person, job to job, place to place. Everybody rather rootless, nobody with a past. And I think that if I had a *vocation*, it would be a kind of lifelong *theme*, act as a *spine*."

"Well, you see that's why the short story is so popular today," said Junie. "What is called the contingency of things, the fragmentation of life, has killed the novel. People live sequentially. You're right. Of course, I don't myself have a stake in believing this, you understand. I like the old form—a story that is almost almond shaped. And it gets its form from the idea that if you start something you've got to finish it . . . you've got that obligation. But of course in life nothing is finished. Have you tried writing short stories?"

"I don't get started on anything. I must lack the passion, you know. I mean I think I have the passion but I don't know what for," Fanny said, uncomfortable now, half-smiling, aware that she was getting the kind attention that belonged to Maryann, if there was a finite supply.

"Passion has a short lease," said Lutécie, suddenly, who thought this conversation was going nowhere. "Do you know Ninon de Lenclos? She was a woman of the seventeenth century, greatly admired for her wit and beauty, and the number of her lovers, and she said to one of them, 'I shall love you for three months. For me that will be an eternity.' " Lutécie smiled and added, "I must associate myself with that remark."

"That's *exactly* what I'm afraid of," said Fanny, laughing.

"I used to think about it a lot, too," said Maryann unexpectedly. "Finally, I thought, you've got to settle on one man and then vow not to veer, like the virgin saints vowed they would be brides of Jesus, and then the vow is sort of *in place* of a vocation. I couldn't see what else to do." She in fact sounded a lot like a saint. They were all surprised to hear what she was thinking, to hear from her at all.

Lutécie said, "Was it our Cecilia, or was it Lucy?—one of those really adamant virgins—they hitched her to a team of oxen to drag her to a brothel, but she *wouldn't budge*."

"It takes that sort of resolution," said the mild Maryann, and something kept Junie's mouth shut. Everybody in fact was silent.

They were delivered by Carrie, who came in triumphant with a *tarte Tatin*, blistering hot. The first one she had tried had stuck to the pan. Titus came after her, to have a piece of it. Everybody said it was absolutely marvelous and everybody burnt his tongue.

Carrie was keeping her eye on Lutécie, uncertain how alarming her problems were. There was in fact a general worry about her, everybody hoping it was only arthritis. They talked for a while about their own symptoms and got cheered by their own survival, and were thereupon able to offer her an optimistic prognosis. Her case was not serious and a lot of pain was all she'd have to suffer. They then turned their attention to Fanny. Fanny had only a week left in France and had seen *nothing*, not even the neighboring restored town of Cordes. There was a general bout of group castigating and volunteers to guide her. Junie said he and Maryann were not willing to go to Cordes but they would be willing, just barely, to go to Conques. In France, whenever any old town or village is rescued from total ruin and restored there is a chorus of contempt for signs that money has been used to do the job. Carrie said that since Titus was going up to Souillac anyway, he could take Fanny to Conques. They could also go on to Rocamadour. Titus, who had previously been warned that this suggestion was going to be made, said nothing then, said nothing now.

Lutécie, squinting first at Titus, then at Fanny, said, "Titus knows every village church, every market, every roadside calvary. If you go with *him*, why, you'll fall in love—with *France*. And if you have a love affair with France, three months would not *be* an *eternity*. What do you think, Titus?" she asked, and repeated the witty remark of Ninon de Lenclos.

"The question, Lu, is equivocal," he said. He looked encroached upon.

Fanny thought Titus didn't at all like the idea of driving

off with her. To rescue him, to rescue them both, she said, "*Eternity*. I know what I wanted to ask you, Titus. Why is a street in the *domaine* of the church called *la rue de la Temporalité?* Why isn't it Eternity?" As she watched him the thought crossed her mind again that he might be gay, and she looked quickly across to Carrie, as if for confirmation, or as if they were a pair of sorts. They seemed to Fanny to be in sympathetic alliance.

"Temporality," Titus said, "only means the church's temporal possessions. It concerns its earthly realm as opposed to its spiritual. In this part of the country the devil has fiercely contested both realms, right down through the centuries. Heretics, Protestants, rebels, Royalists—the devil is everywhere. Either Paris is his instrument, or Rome. In Souillac there's a spendid twelfth-century Isaiah I'm using just inside the church door, brought in during the revolution so that it wouldn't be destroyed." This carried Titus to the very brink of an invitation to drive up to see it. He stopped short of that. He was having a wrestle with a private devil of his own. His devil was a coward, a craven-hearted, nothing-ventured-nothing-lost doom-warner. ever amatory prospects threatened Titus this devil saved him from them. Fanny was not actually very threatening.

Carrie was annoyed at the resisting Titus. With a small toss of her head, she turned to Fanny, and said, "There's a wonderful story Mistral's father tells about the revolution, and an eccentric old woman who lives at the edge of their village. Riquelle, her name is. It was at the time of the Terror, and of course all the feast days and the masses on Sundays had been abolished. And instead, every tenth day everybody gathered with great pomp to worship the Goddess of Reason. At that time Riquelle was about eighteen, the freshest, prettiest girl in the village, and there she was, dressed as a goddess, thigh half-bare, a breast uncovered, the *bonnet rouge* on her head, sitting in this costume on the altar of the church."

"Not always a very *sensuous* goddess, you know," said Lutécie a little mechanically. She and Carrie were very familiar with each other's stories.

It was sensuous enough for Titus. He said, "If you like, Fanny, I'll show you the sort of church it was," lured over the brink by the titillating Goddess of Reason.

Seventeen

On monday Fanny got up with the dawn, the first dawn
with a sun, and the sun was to shine through this excellent
week. "I think the sun has taken an interest in having our
excursions successful," said Fanny to Titus, as they took
off on one of these mornings. "I am reminded of Madame
Bovary. Do you remember when she's having the terribly
sinful affair and she says to Rodolphe that she thinks their
two mothers in heaven are looking down and blessing their
union? I like that sort of cosmic involvement."

Titus and Fanny were certainly not having a love affair,
and she was entirely easy about making this reference.
Indeed her happiness rested on the desexualized nature of
the fellowship she felt with Titus. It was as well for Titus
that he didn't know that.

They had Carrie's little Renault and they would set off
early, to the accompaniment of France Musique, the clas-
sical station. They would begin to lose it on one band and
pick it up clearly on another, entirely unlike one's experience twenty minutes out of Boston when it sounds as
though the Russians are jamming even Tchaikovsky.

France Musique, moreover, took American jazz as solemnly as Telemann and Bach. That week it was really into Judy Garland, who was also involved with the weather ("I'm gonna love you like nobody loves you/Come rain or come shine"). Titus and Fanny sang along. Mysteriously Titus knew all the songs. By the last of their five days they had covered a surprisingly little area of the map—they never even saw Rocamadour—but had gotten a "Ding, ding, ding, went the trolley" duet going that was of nearly professional quality.

They made the slowest sort of progress, parked in every village, looked in its church, bought fruit in its market, drew to the side of every stream, every calvary, many without any interest at all. They were driving through the Causses, a limestone plateau, the fields sparse, hardly enough vegetation for one cow. Three times they saw one cow walking in a field, with a woman following it, knitting. "I've got to get wool," said Fanny. "I notice there are a lot of wool shops in Albi. And then when I get back to New York, all I'll need is a cow. It's a good combination. You can't just sit and knit."

"One cow can represent tremendous security. Nadezhda Mandelstam thought if she could get a cow it would keep them safe from Stalin," said Titus reflectively. Whatever came up, he could reflect on it.

They were in the abbey church in Souillac. Although Fanny had not previously known of the existence of the reliefs and the Isaiah, or even of Souillac (and for that matter, although she had not read Mandelstam) she wasn't now made frantic by the immensity of her ignorance, as she had been on first seeing the Lautrecs. This wandering inch by inch through places she'd never heard of had a pacifying effect on the kind of anxiety that springs up in many people in Florence or Paris, for instance, when they think they might be looking at the wrong Fra Angelico, walking through the wrong rooms of the Louvre. They aren't Philistines. It is panic engendered by how much they don't know, and how short the time is in which to get started. Titus, meanwhile, continued to know everything. He said, "These reliefs were mutilated by the Protestants in the Religious wars. Your great grandmother came from the mutilating Protestants, something Carrie finds very comforting."

"Do you mean from right here?"

"She's never found out just where, but she's said it was a feeling of affinity that brought her to focus on Provençal, on Mistral, and in the end to set up housekeeping in Albi."

"That grandmother was barely literate. Carrie says when she was little she used to read to her after school, books like the Bobbsey Twins."

"I come from rabbis and rednecks. It has crossed my mind that my maternal grandfather never did learn his letters. Numbers he learned. He had to count his money."

The next day they were in a small twelfth-century church, nobody around, and Fanny asked, "I suppose you don't know what it was exactly that brought about Carrie's leaving Boston? I thought of her as abandoning us. It was very painful."

"Well, I *know* she certainly came to a critical point with Mistral."

"Mistral? I can't believe my father was worried about *Mistral.* I can't believe he ever heard of him. *I* never heard of him. I thought he was a *wind.*"

"She says that she took a six-month leave to come to Provence to do a book on Mistral, and halfway along she thought she had to know more about what else was going on in the middle of the nineteenth century. So she began reading Alexander Herzen, *My Life and Thoughts*, and that did it! She found she couldn't go back to Mistral. It was just one of those intellectual crises. It's very common. You either get over it or you don't. Those who don't play the market take up golf. Now Carrie with the Printing House to support her was into what you call a good combination, like knitting and tending the cow. She was no longer historically *confined* either by the need to teach or to write. She could range at will—I think of her as in charge of the centuries—and of course she reads for review."

"Also I never heard of whoever *that* was," Fanny said, half to herself, meaning Herzen, but not sounding annoyed.

"I'd like to see you sitting on that altar. You'd make a first-rate Goddess of Reason. You're just the right shape," said Titus. He did think Fanny would make a first-rate goddess of whatever, and he was sure she didn't want to hear about Herzen. Fanny laughed and danced out of the empty church.

They went on to Conques, singing, or bellowing,

> "When you're laughing,
> When you're laughing,
> The sun comes shining through,"

another weather song.

"I like Conques because I like little children," said Titus. The relics of Ste Foye, a child saint, were in Conques. They had climbed up through the winding streets of the little town, a pilgrim stop on the route to Compostela. It was a mild afternoon, and in late October there was only a scattering of tourists, or pilgrims. One place was open for coffee, filled with flies, and there Fanny and Titus talked, their arms waving, fending them off.

"Ste Foye was a little girl of quite steadfast devotion. They broiled her, they grilled her—she wouldn't give up," said Titus. "They don't make children like that any more. There was another baby so holy that he refused the breast on Sundays and feast days. Improbable as it seems, I'd like to have children. I even liked Cordelia and Lucia when they were small."

"Your sisters definitely daunt me," said Fanny, after a moment. She could not say, Why improbable, she thought.

"Jesus, they daunt everybody. They have the curious *moral* conviction that if they do what they want to do they are adding to the sum total of the happiness of mankind. Regular *benefactors*. Now they've brought those two babies home and for unfathomable reasons, neither my mother nor my father is expressing some of that happiness. My mother's resilient, but my father, my poor father . . ."

"Your *father* daunts me," said Fanny.

Titus was quiet and then he said, "You know if you're a Jew life can be a real tug of war. A real hassle." Both his arms were swinging and he might have hit seven flies. "Sometimes it does seem to come down to a name. I have a cousin, Stephen Sidney Stein, grew up in Minneapolis, cut off the Stephen, named his children Eli and Miriam, and went to live in Israel. My father grew up in Minneapolis and cut off the Stein. The reason he dropped it was because he did not want to be endowed by others with loyalties and beliefs they thought he should have." He looked at Fanny mildly and was wondering whether to proceed. He went on, "After Hannah Arendt wrote her book on Eichmann she was accused of betraying 'her people.' It made her mad as hell. She said nobody was to tell her who *her people* were.

She chose *her people*. My father's never managed with that élan. He always suspects somebody's ready to say Ah-ha! It makes him waspish." Titus grinned. "If you don't go shacking up with a lot of women, people assume you don't like women," he threw in.

They both remained silent for some minutes.

"Do you feel you've been denied a heritage?" Fanny asked, reverting to the Jewish question.

"No. *Amor fati.* No, I like the way my lot fell out. I like being an observer instead of a believer. I'm glad I'm my father's son—instead of his brother's."

"I don't know why I worry about *your* heritage. We haven't had any religion since we gave up mutilating."

Titus wasn't finished: "I dodge certain responsibilities but I take on others. Somewhere Joseph Brodsky says 'Liberté, égalité, fraternité . . . why does nobody add *culture?*' Now there is the obviously dismaying fact that as you move towards egalitarianism, you get anti-intellectualism. Everything is a trade-off. Well, I'd like to . . . honor the canons of Western culture, and at the same time remain a lovable social democrat . . . You've got to work both sides of the street. Carrie believes that to make the most responsible possible citizen, you have to have a really private life to think in. And what you think in private will often conflict with what, sometimes, you must in fact *do*, in public. A really exemplary decent citizen is going to be filled with misgivings."

"So *that's* what I am, exemplary."

The days passed and they went on with their singing, moving from the subject of weather to the subject of health. ("You go to my head/With a smile that makes my temperature rise.")

At one point Fanny asked Titus whether he thought Carrie would return home even if Lutécie decided to stay. Titus looked at her oddly, as though it were a fatuous question or disingenuous, and said only that Carrie would never leave Lutécie. She felt herself redden.

Fanny, meanwhile, had a new list—French Villages I Have Walked In—which was getting quite long. Since lists are one of the things scholars make, Titus did not, as TX had, think Fanny might be kinky on this ground. And Fanny had not confided the existence of her master Finest People list to Titus because of not wanting to hear what candidates he had to offer. She was also worried that he would know something about Marcus Aurelius or Keats that would be disqualifying. The list was already very short. But on their last half day, after they had spent the morning in Castres and were celebrating with a grand lunch on Titus, in Réalmont, she pulled out this list.

Titus looked at it, seeming bemused. After a moment, he said "Once when I was in Rome I went up to see the room where Keats died. It was a building right off the bottom of the Spanish Steps. Three rooms, actually, and they sell Keats-Shelley ashtrays." He grinned and they ate. He was not at all inclined to contribute to her private list. He had a private list of his own, a lubricious list, in cipher in case he died unexpectedly.

Another health song they sang, a mental-health song, was 'This can't be love because I feel so well,/No sobs, no sorrows, no sighs,' although Titus had definitely by now begun wondering whether it was really a health song after all, but because he was so susceptible to, or because he was so ignobly timid in the sight of, women, he did not suggest to Fanny the possible alternative meaning this song might have for him. Every opportunity to mention this he let fly by.

As for Fanny, she was in ferment, heart and soul, night and day, and she was in love, was in love, was in love with Carrie, with Lutécie, with Junie and Maryann, with Alain, as well as with Titus. Charged up to the ears with the impressions of two French weeks, she was terribly reluctant to leave—although she was returning to a broke and jobless situation, oddly with a sanguine spirit. Friday night at her last dinner she was hugged by her new lifelong dear friends, and went up with Carrie vaguely aware how quickly replaceable she was in their thoughts.

Carrie brought out two snifters and they drank brandy.

"Well, what do you think? How was it with Titus?"

"I'm absolutely punchy with information. Do I look smarter?"

"I mean seriously. *I* love Titus." Carrie waited. She thought Fanny ought to love Titus.

Fanny could not say that she loved Titus, afraid to use the word breezily, afraid to use it at all. Her emotions were in an undiscussable tangle. Finally she said, "It's what Lutécie predicted. I'm having a love affair with France."

Carrie thought Fanny minded Titus's failure to be tall, dark, and handsome.

Eighteen

YOU'RE coming home. You've made up your mind?"
Fanny asked.

"Yes."

"I already love it here. I'm on the side of Lu and Junie."

"I'm homesick. Isn't it funny? I'm impatient to be back.
I miss B Street when the seasons change—when life moves
outside to the porches. It's as though we were part of the
great eternal rhythm of the flocks, moving from winter to
summer pasture—a transhumance."

"We don't even have the house any more!"

"Well, and I also need to rally to our side, to the side of
the self-slaughtering Democrats . . ." She smiled. Her
mind meandered. "This could be a very interesting time for
political *rethinking*, you know, Fanny, and lately, here in
France, I've been feeling a little dispossessed . . . disarmed.
I look at the tricolor and I think that's not the right flag. I
don't entertain the belief that my going back will turn the
country around *immediately*," Carrie said, and looked for a
moment defeated in advance. The truth was that people
attributed to Carrie a lot more cheerful optimism than she

herself had the pleasure of enjoying. "And I've got to make the move *now*, while I still have the energy to get this group moving—against the westerlies. The last time I changed course I remember having titanic feelings of competence, of being welcomed to the company of giants, *belonging* with them. Well, I don't have all that now."

Carrie had told Fanny about meeting Lutécie in Cannes but had stopped at the water's edge. She had stopped because of a dilemma with several points on its horns, those points of integrity that were *in situ* in the middle-class world of B Street fifteen years ago. Fifteen years ago divorce was shocking; love affairs were shocking; infidelity, betrayal, virginity, responsibility, honor, still serious words.

"You know, fifteen years ago one knew, even on B Street, that the structure of ethical assumptions was buckling, and one certainly had reason to wonder what would be left in the course of time. But there *was* no course of time. It sunk like a stone. To you our compunctions must seem in the category of the quaint, like those that did in Hetty Sorrel or Hester Prynne."

"Oh, I don't know. To have a strong principle override a strong desire sounds rather invigorating. Even to have a strong desire . . ."

"I was thirty-five before things began to come together for me, Fanny." It was Fanny now. "I didn't like your being Fanny because I thought it meant you were taking yourself too flippantly."

"But I don't, I suppose," said Fanny wryly.

"No."

"My mother said when you came back from France they'd got another Carrie from the one they'd sent out."

"Well, they did. That's right. I came back in a sort of

. . . *hospitable* state. That's how I think of it now. One always distorts the past, of course. But I'd gone off to France a disciplined academic with a sure sense of direction, intent upon cultivating a certain field, securing a certain modest place, in a known field, and I came back scrappy, even *litigious*. For one thing I was no longer interested in anything *modest*. For another, the whole stretch of the six months of trekking through Provence was rushing madly out of consequence. My mind would keep straying to that one day in Cannes. I kept trying to retrieve the possibilities implied in the conversation with Lu, whoever Lu might be. I began scanning the women's page of the *Times* and even the obituaries, and the more there was no mention of this Lu, the more possessed I became of the need to track her down. Actually I'd no sooner said good-bye to them that afternoon when I swore at my craven self for not asking them to say again who they were. I wandered down to the boats to see whether I could find theirs, which was called *Innocent*, and sure enough, finally, there it was, looking very much like every other yacht—and not handsome like a sailing ship—*Innocent III*, Portsmouth, it said among all the others registered in Nice. *Innocent III!* I thought. What crust. Or did it mean that the two previous *Innocent*s had sunk to the bottom of the sea?

"Anyway, I saw the meeting with Lu as a portent, you know, something in the nature of three eagles flying over the head—a larky promise for a future of an altogether unexpected ten best years ahead. And I was ready for it."

Meanwhile, once she was back in Cambridge, she could not give all her time to this mind drifting. She had to prepare for classes, and moreover, she had been greeted at the airport like a conquered heroine by her family, who assigned her new battles to fight. This family was promoting Black Power and the withdrawal of the American presence in Southeast Asia. The pace of change, however, was unsatisfactory (the citizens of Massachusetts always find) and Marcus thought he would run for Congress, what did Carrie think? "And you wrapped your arms around me to insure my thinking *right*, and I said wonderful, and was immediately assigned Cambridge and the conscripting of my friends."

"I remember the green velvet coat, and your hair done up, and your neck so long. We thought you looked like a beautiful duchess."

"My neck was always cold that winter. I wondered why I didn't have chronic sore throat. But for the first time in my life I felt successfully *feminine*—not docile. Quite the contrary. I was becoming, in fact, what turned out to be a feminist. And meanwhile my Cambridge world was in ferment, not altogether attractive at the time. In fact curiously . . . fretful."

Carrie's friends had been grouped in the old style, either married colleagues-and-their-wives or single women. They all, it seemed, had used her time away to disrupt their lives. There were separations. There was a rash of sleeping with students, an unprecedented breach of trust in the academic world (and of all the hallowed mores in that world destined to reverse themselves, none would do so in such blanket fashion). Most instructive for Carrie was humble and genteel Christine Smith, who had decided to apply for tenure. "You can tell your brother," she had said, biting her words, "that women are the largest oppressed minority in the world, nowhere more patronized than in the universities, and if he's prepared to make our civil rights a plank I'll support him, and if he isn't he can go to hell in a handbasket."

"This was my first roar of feminist fury," said Carrie to Fanny, "and coming from a previous mouse. I was angry at first about her disloyalty. But I was amazed to find how quickly I would share her preoccupation. Do you know how many women had tenure that year? One. And if Christine had the extravagant luck of winning a place, that used up the whole supply of extravagant luck.

"So I tracked down your father, which was difficult to do, and I said, 'A lot of people think you could add a major plank to your platform.' and I explained to him the problems of women in the academic world.

"And he had a man's genius for figures and quickly calculated that women in academic life were not an interesting bloc of votes. Of course *later*, he really came round.

"The other thing I had on my mind was the yacht. I mentioned, in the briefest way, the lovely lunch and wanting to write a note of thanks. And I had assumed Portsmouth, *England*, was meant—all their boats on their side, all our boats on our side, you know? But it had just occurred to me that it was under an *American* flag, and so it might be *New Hampshire*, and there must be a registry, and could he find out his name?"

"Perfectly easy," Marcus had said. "*Innocent III*, ha! Easy to remember. Portsmouth. No trouble at all."

"I'd just be awfully anxious to . . ." had said his effusive sister.

"No trouble at all. Forget it," had said Marcus with a wave of his hand, and he forgot it.

Several times in the weeks that followed Marcus had called Carrie, always on the fly, always with instructions involving his campaign, and when she once ventured to remind him of her yacht problem, he said, in an apologetic voice, "Oh Jesus! I haven't had a minute, but I'll get to it."

"To put things fairly," said Carrie to Fanny, "I had not followed any of your father's instructions about his congressional campaign. 'Carrie,' he'd order, 'I want you to think about making a list of women who'll stuff envelopes.' I did not think about a list. I had become balky on policy, and was actively looking for things to balk about. Only in regard to the univerisity where I was diddling for that promotion did I remain a patsy." Otherwise, so abstracted, so dreamy had she been, shuttling back and forth to B Street, head high, undisturbed by transit breakdowns, by blizzards that swirled around her naked neck, she'd often thought it was miraculous to find herself, like a milkman's horse, meeting her appointments on time, her classes prepared. Her apartment in the thread mill, its windows overhanging the snow-banked half-frozen stream which was glinting and tumbling and looking not at all like an open sewer, she had once found charming, a retreat. She now thought, a retreat, not charming. "To which," she said to Fanny, "I was nonetheless returning one afternoon when there was Will Costello heading off towards the foot bridge. I hadn't seen him since I'd gotten back, and at the very sight of him I thought, *Boats, he* might know."

Will Costello had been known in Carrie's time, and was still known in Fanny's, as a man of arcane knowledge to whom all repaired when there was a problem with gaskets, cutworms, bats, carburetors. He seemed always available, with an office in a thread-mill building, always divertible, working a leisurely twelve hours a day. At night he must have heard, "Say Will, you got a minute?" in his sleep. He had a boat.

"I really hadn't *known* him," said Carrie to Fanny. "I mean, I *liked* him. Everybody liked him—a man of the fewest possible words and the most possible children, and more or less hag ridden, you know—Faye ran the house, Faye ran the office. She did *not* have time for fooling around."

"I liked her because when they were choosing up for volleyball she made them include girls," said Fanny, fair but uneasy.

"Anyhow, we went back to his office and he poured two water glasses of whisky. He said something about my selfless brother's going off to fight for the downtrodden, and I said something like selfless egomaniac, and then I told him about the yacht . . . In fact I told him a lot about France and that day in Cannes. He's wonderful to talk to, he draws you on . . . and I remember I only got nervous about *Innocent III* because he was a Catholic and I was concerned he might be offended. I said that he was thought to be a good pope, you know, in order to mitigate . . ." Carrie laughed. She had a taste for this memory. It was warming her up. "Well, he didn't say anything, and he got up and poked around through the clutter and found what he wanted, some sort of nautical almanac, and he riffled through it, jotting down things, all the while never a word. And then he dialed a number and said to me, 'Portsmouth'—that's all—and then the next thing he was explaining with absolutely sonorous authority that he had to trace the ownership of this yacht. Well, he got a lot of flack at the other end, you could hear. And then he bellowed, 'Nondivulgent policy! Madame, this is Frederick O. Quinn, Quinn Levine Foote, Boston attorneys for James T. Shea, Harbormaster, Smuggling Division. We must have this information immediately.' And evidently the person went off to see, and he held the phone waiting, and I said, 'I think the last time I saw you was at Mr. Quinn's funeral.'

" 'That's right. Matter of association,' he said, rather pleased with his performance. But *I* couldn't have been

more *surprised* . . ." Carrie paused to think how to describe
him further.

Fanny said, "Mr. Costello is the other choice of your
. . . relationship."

"*Relationship,*" Carrie said, brought up short. "That's
another ruined word. What fake attention to propriety *that*
means to suggest. At least *gay* adds some cheer, some
humor . . ." She spoke irritably while she was thinking that
her problem right along had been to make her own
transgression reasonable without naming a transgressee.

Fanny retreated to the subject of the yacht and said,
"Well, did Mr. Costello get the name?"

"Well, sure, it was Bennie, of course. That's how I found
Lu. She was the portent . . . and I was captivated by her
. . . One never knows to what extent one contributes, one
forces a portent to prove true . . ." Carrie found her spirits
suddenly deflated. She lost interest in trudging through the
whole silly business. Fanny sensed this and was uncomfortable and quiet. They had a little more brandy. Then
Carrie said, "Actually *love affair* sounds rather dated,
doesn't it? And it isn't synonymous with 'relationship' in
any case. If I ask you if you've ever had a relationship, it's
rather different from asking you if you've ever had a love
affair, isn't it? [pause] Have you?" Carrie was now smiling,
and had restored herself by shifting the strain to Fanny.

"Which?" asked Fanny, amused.

"Well, there's a measure of the changing times! I think
I'll choose love affair. Have you had a love affair?"

Fanny considered the question, felt wistful, shook her
head a little, and said, "I guess not." After a moment, her
tongue loosened by the brandy, she lifted her chin and with
a comic, teasing smile, she asked, "Now, did you have a
love affair?"

"I had a love affair," said Carrie in a low happy voice. What possessed her to say this, after all the circumspection, all the years of discretion, was that she thought they both understood that the subject was a worthwhile love. She thought that implicit in Fanny's response was the acknowledgement of sexual experience, and with a maternal rush of feeling, she wanted to help Fanny set her sights higher; to judge, to weigh, to reflect, to delay, to wait for a worthwhile love.

Nineteen

Lutécie had been lucky in Ben. "Bennie is a loner who
wants the hum of undifferentiated people around him, and
a place to go, you know, in case of Christmas," was how
Lutécie had described him at the time she was preparing to
take off. "He'd really like a life of *dropping by*, you know—
not staying." A true and fortunate predilection for Lutécie
on the one hand, Ben on the other.

Fanny rolled her nose around her brandy glass. She did
not mention that Lutécie was the third candidate for Carrie's love.

"When I got her on the telephone at Kittery it was like
throwing her a rope," said Carrie.

That year Bennie had been interested to rescue his ship
chandler's firm, obliging Lutécie to spend more of the winter in Maine than was to her taste. After the call from Carrie she had ventured bravely south to Boston, a drive from
Kittery not much more than an hour, and settled in to the
the Ritz. Boston took her breath away. She discovered it as
though it had been previously under a bushel, and back
from a walk, back from a museum, would look at Carrie

with something like awe for having carried the thing off so well.

"Did you think it was a clearing in the wood?" I asked her.

She crossed the river for a panoramic view and believed there was never such a red brick city piled on a hill, but as it turned out fate would bring her to Albi and that would be another. She saw its paintings, listened to its music, adored Sarah Caldwell, and all this redounded to Carrie's credit.

"I was captivated by Lu, by the Ritz, where I had eaten twice in my entire life, but in the beginning I didn't know what impelled her towards somebody like me. I knew she had said in Cannes that she wanted to be free of the role of consort, a baffling remark in all ways beyond my comprehension—of course *since*, one's heard a lot about that. But *then* I thought that at her age she'd be ready for some conventional settling down. After all, she was fifty-four, older than I am now, but"—and here Carrie turned a little dreamy and her voice got silvery—"I have to say she looked ageless, with those lovely oval green eyes, like a more *sanguine* Virginia Woolf—or even a Virginia Woolf who *sang*. It was so funny and at the same time absolutely *commanding* to watch her strike through the two creamy buff rooms of her suite, in billowing blue silk, with that *sprezzatura*, singing arias from *Der Rosenkavalier*, for the therapeutic reason that it buoyed her spirits. I was always expecting knocking on the walls."

"She says she sings to think."

"Exactly, and she was thinking of wriggling out of her rather complicated obligations, and where to get the money. That's why she looked at the unanticipated inheritance of the Printing House as such a windfall. It was a guarantor of her independence. Well, and then the inheritance was *contested*. Bennie certainly would have seen to the lawyers and so on, but there was this conjoining of events in Lu's life too, as well as in mine. By my being able to produce your father, it kept her side tidier.

"Your *father*. First he didn't have a split second to spare. But once he'd met her, well, he simply threw himself into the business. It was settled in some kind of international record time. She dazzled him. He'd go trotting over to the Ritz whenever she was in town . . . You know if he weren't such a straight arrow, and if Lutécie hadn't been intent upon retiring from the field, so to speak—but he was the last of a breed, I guess." Carrie said this with unwavering certainty. Her overestimation of her brother's moral fortitude was entirely sincere. She hadn't a notion, when she went off with Lutécie, of saving Marcus from an act of dishonor.

"She even dazzled David Sidney, difficult to do," said Carrie. "I brought him to meet her. I thought he would be intrigued."

"And Alison? Was Alison intrigued?"

"Alison was busy. Listen, Fanny, anybody wanting a long marriage needs a lot of space."

"I'm only laughing. I'm just surprised you were so freewheeling—in those old-fashioned days."

"Well, it's true that I found myself somewhat . . . loosened, but I tell you flatly I was *not* freed from a sense of moral judgment. And, moreover, you do an injustice if you dismiss David. David is a strange man, but very learned, very principled. It's difficult to know him but it's altogether worthwhile. Titus has been fortunate in his father."

"He thinks so."

"The reason I got to know David so well was because he

supported my bid for tenure—the only yea vote—without even letting me know. He was a feminist of the first quality, possibly the only one I've ever known. Of course he's a *humanist* of the first quality. He was fond of quoting Eliot: tradition 'cannot be inherited, and if you want it you must obtain it by great labor.' "

"Did you love him?"

"Did I love him? Of course I loved him, but in those days one did not sleep with everybody one loved, a failure to act that now, I suppose, sounds archaic," she said, a little testy. She was giving herself airs. Nothing human was alien to her as well as the next woman. That lust-filled year she was attracted to all sorts of men and curiously, even alarmingly, they to her. It was as though her body had suddenly begun producing musk. She did not have a sordid tale to tell, by the skin of her teeth.

"You know, what I *really remember*," said Fanny, feeling entitled to pursue this subject, "on that day in Rockport, when we were feeding the gulls, and you told me that you were in love . . . what I really *remember* is your *sound* of being entirely, surely, certain. It was a deliriously happy sound. And I have never heard it again. I don't even *know* a woman who hasn't had *something* going . . . some man . . . and now, even when a lot of people have begun getting married . . . but I have never heard any woman talk about being in love with that certainty, or with that crazy *happiness* . . ."

"Well, it was so *unexpected*. It was queer . . ." Carrie stopped, disconcerted, wondering where the moral of the tale could be found.

"What do you mean queer?" Fanny asked abruptly.

"I think, looking back, that the circumstances in my life then, and the sort of rules that pertained then, rules of permissible behavior, rules of discretion . . ." She paused to change course. "Really the thing that charmed me out of my senses, that *overwhelmed* me, was being loved by a person of such unconventional assumptions. It was that inch-by-inch awakening to another person's perception of propriety, of how life must be ordered. It was the factor of surprise." Carrie tried to remember what was surprising, but could not. "I just can't see how any tension can build today. There's never anything allowed to stay unknown for long enough. And what conventions are left? I fell in love so unpredictably. It probably accounts for the intensity."

"Was it Lutécie?" Out it came. Fanny, stoical, looked straight at her straight-backed aunt.

"*Lutécie?* So that's what they were after, that gang at *First.*" She was exasperated. "I have to say the sexual bullying, the intimidation and blackmailing is the nastiest excrescence of the feminist movement. They let one kind of woman out of the closet and shove another kind in. They've got to have a closet." She needed a deep breath. "I can't tell you how companionable it is to live with a woman *because* there is so little sexual tension. Surely many women through the ages have recognized this pleasant fate. It really seems spiteful, this rewriting of history . . . the vulgar recasting of old friendships. For God's sake when I say unusual or unexpected, I'm talking about the features of a *mind* not a body. I fell in love with somebody because of what he *thought*, what made him *laugh*. I was just altogether surprised who he was, that's all!"

Fanny was a child of her times up to a point. That the love was conventional, just for a man, left her weak with relief. She was distressed that it mattered so much. If she had herself been a lesbian she would have been distressed the other way, and would have lost a feasible projection of the kind of woman she would like to head toward being. Vaguely she hoped she would have risen above her smaller self, and in the meanwhile there was no need to bother. Now she wondered which man it was, seesawing between David Sidney and Mr. Costello. She did not ask. She went all the way back to New York City not knowing. All Carrie said about the dénouement of this affair was that they had gone to the movies together, way off in Framingham where nobody would know them, and as they were coming out, there was Marcus. She couldn't cope with her sense of shame. Whether she could today, under the new dispensation, she couldn't tell. She did not name the movie or the man.

The movie had been *Casablanca*, an old cult film even then. If they'd walked out of *Annie Hall* or *Manhattan*, where a lot of poor devils move mournfully from bed to bed, everybody a *little* disappointed, nobody *quite* right, her life might never have taken the turn it did. She might have bluffed it through with Marcus. Not fled. And there was a certain embarrassment in having to admit that one's conscience was put in turmoil by watching Ingrid Bergman give up Humphrey Bogart, something she did not in fact admit, either to Fanny on the eve of her leaving Albi, nor at the time to Will.

She had been overwhelmed by Will. After all, it depends upon who you are. Will wasn't likely to have overwhelmed the Marquis de Sade. But if Fanny had been a child of her times, so was everybody. Carrie grew up in a family of almost Emersonian chastity. Her father and mother, whatever their private reservations, had led her to understand that almost everybody obeyed the most stringent sexual rules, through history, through time, through societies, and in Boston in particular. Of course it is the sort of proposition one begins to inspect from the moment one has a toe through the school door, and especially high-school door. And Carrie didn't have to wait until she fell into Will's arms to be disabused of this spirit of wholehearted obedience. Will coming from a Catholic working-class family, never having been steeped in the above lore, was widely respected, known to be a man of his word. But he observed another order of moral obligation, simple enough and familiar, but in Will Carrie saw it in the flesh, so to speak. It was a kind of ethics of dependability. He kept his bargains with life. He was a responsible husband, father, church member, businessman, neighbor, citizen, and when these performances did not correspond to his private feeling, he found himself annoyed, sometimes even enraged, but not conflicted. He was not troubled by hypocrisy. He accepted this division in himself without angst, and in fact had never thought about it. He made love to Carrie with a truly untroubled conscience. He was comfortable in his own skin, as the French put it.

But of course it was Will's skin, and Carrie was not comfortable in it. She foreswore her love and her renouncement proved as painful as it was supposed to be, and moreoever and alas, she never felt the better woman for the renunciation. It was a long time before she gave up fantasies of Will's turning up in Albi, of her being startled by the sight of him coming around the rue de la Temporalité. No possibility of that at all. He'd never even been east of Provincetown. And she hadn't to this day stopped loving the memory of this almost parodic paterfamilias, this archetype of the leaf-raking, churchgoing father of six sons—they needed two cars to go to mass on Sunday—notwithstanding he was an unbeliever ("I must say I'm surprised. I'm sure everybody thinks you are a devout Catholic." "Nobody ever asked me, one way or the other."), notwithstanding he disliked his wife ("Do you think of leaving her?" "I try not to think of her at all."). She certainly had laughed from one end of the four months to the other, a mindlessly passionate affair, every hour stolen, grateful that there were four months, and that they hadn't gone to see *Casablanca* at the beginning. And she never knew that Marcus hadn't seen them.

Afterwards they had exchanged letters of a formal nature. Then last year after Faye died Will sent her a post-card of a Greek vase from the Museum of Fine Arts. It said: "Winding down the Thread Mill." From those words, the need to return home took hold, and there ensued a rapid correspondence in postcards, hers wondering if a thread mill could be turned into a Printing House, his getting esti-mates, hers that she couldn't come up with that kind of money, interest at 20 percent, and by return mail, "Sure you can, with a sleeping partner, Figuratively, Will."

Twenty

Back in New York Fanny had no more than greeted
Missy, for whom two weeks wasn't all that long a time,
than she believed she could not endure being thought of as
the same person she had been and that went for Missy twice
over. Hardly had they finished squealing, clutching, and
kissing than Fanny snapped, "Just don't ask me if anybody's gay, okay?" Missy thought she'd be goddamned if
she'd ask her anything at all, and in this way Fanny might
have resumed her life quietly. But instead they made allow-
ances for Fanny's jet lag, as it was kindly put, and discussed, with some formality, prospects for Fanny's
immediate future, which included being fired and not having her share of the rent money.

On the telephone to her mother and father Fanny was
extravagant and theatrical, giving them no reason to think
they'd gotten back another daughter from the one they'd
sent out. "And the upshot is, daddy, that I'm in a 'Do-not-
pass-go, do-not-collect-$200' employment situation," she
said, awfully cute, shriveling, but also baffled by where her
confident maturity could have gone to, that French amour

propre you get in France. ("It doesn't travel," said Missy.)
Marcus said reasonably, "Now, let's see. You owe *First*
what? You figure it out and then calculate how much you'll
need to carry you through the next stretch until you find
something, and I'll send along a check to cover you." Fanny
bridled silently, obeying what is called in political science
the Law of Colonial Ingratitude.

She had Sunday to shake off the flight and prepare for
her interview with Candace. Missy, prohibited from men-
tioning the pivotal question regarding Foote and Tavernier,
was silent when asked for help.

"The thing is, I really don't want it (meaning sexual pref-
erence) to make any difference," said Fanny, pleading for a
little understanding. "I really admire her very much . . ."

"So she *is* gay."

"No, she *isn't!* That's what I mean! And I'd just like not
to give Candace the satisfaction of knowing the truth.
And on the other hand she already thinks she knows it
and I'd just like to fling a wet flounder across her face . . .
Do you know, I never had such wonderful fish. They
served it a lot. Of course in the back of your mind you just
hope they got them from some pure and crystal spring instead of the river—skimming them dead off the top. But in
France it's better not to ask. The government is amazingly
autocratic for a democracy, Titus says. And of course it
tastes absolutely delicious, whatever . . . But if I could walk
in there in a *soigné* way—I'm going to dress for this part—
and tell her I find it impossible to *breach*, to *dishonor*, the
canons of privacy, of integrity . . ."

"Who's Titus?"

"Oh, just a guy."

"Well, maybe she won't fire you. If you're going to give

her back what they laid out, I don't see she has the *right* . . ."

Fanny, ten counterthoughts traveling through her head like bewildered bugs, said only, "I want to get out of there."

"Was he French?"

"Teetoos?" Fanny laughed, and said, "You'd be fascinated by Alain, Alain Grossepatte. You think you are in Xanadu and then you meet Alain and you think you've never left Amsterdam Avenue. His *hero* is Woody Allen. He thinks New York is filled with people like that. I was really disappointing. And guess what? He's getting his advanced degree in sociology and he came down to the Printing House to study American expatriates, how they behave. Actually, it's not as dopey as you think . . . although *Titus* is certainly dismissive. He thinks Alain's trained to observe certain specific things, to count how many there are, and misses almost everything else. Titus has absurdly high standards. It's incredible."

"Who's Titus?"

"Nobody, really."

"The other nobody called. He said he forgot when you were due back."

"Is that so?" Fanny said, her voice carrying mild interest, careful not to give herself away. She was in fact concealing confusion above all from herself, but also from Missy, in order to avoid being straightened out. And of course in regard to Missy she had found herself back in the same awkward bind of being fortunate but not deserving. More so, since one can scarcely come back from one's first trip to France disappointed. About France Fanny thought she should sound a touch ironic, instead of a touch obsessed.

Although the truth was that almost every moment of her trip was at once a revelation and a conundrum, almost every thought of it bringing her stock-still. She was wary of parading this, for Missy's sake, although the only way she could brazen out the fantastic clothes Maryann Waterman had handed down to her was not wear them, and she wasn't into that sort of sacrifice.

Fanny walked into Candace's office on Monday morning looking smashing in these clothes, although Candace did not betray her astonishment.

"Welcome back. How'd it go?" Candace asked, smiling very pleasantly.

Fanny was at once thrown into confusion: "I'm sorry to disappoint you," she said stiffly, "but it's just one of those circumstances about which it would be improper to write a story. It couldn't be done without a gross invasion of privacy. I'm making arrangements to reimburse you for my expenses, but I . . . ."

"No, we'll absorb that. I had a hunch it wouldn't work but it was worth a try. I hope at least you got some fun out of it," said Candace, with a hitherto unsuspected best of humor, casting Fanny's carefully prepared defense into disarray. It was absolutely whimsical of Candace to take such a setback so easily. Titus said that tyrants are whimsical, a way to keep people off balance. Stalin was whimsical.

Fanny said, "I want to say that they aren't lesbians. That's not the issue."

"I wasn't all that convinced myself."

Now Fanny was really off balance and also angry. She said, "In any case, I plan to leave. I'm giving notice."

"Probably wise," said Candace, who could turn on a dime.

Fanny left the office wondering if there was some way she could challenge Candace to a duel. On the other hand, her report of this two-minute interview that evening left Missy wonderfully mollified.

And TX called Fanny even before Fanny was going to call him. He had something on his mind and would she meet him for dinner on Friday. She said she had no job and no money and he said Perfect. So off she went wrapped in Maryann's black spring-weight shawl, the last day of October, Halloween, and froze.

"How did your aunt check out?" They were settled with their chopsticks at a table at a Chinese restaurant on East Forty-fourth Street. She had chattered on about France, about Candace, and he had watched her quizzically, holding his story back.

"Oh, we're really reunited and she told me that her father, my grandfather Foote—that he died on All Hallows Eve and that it was a friendly time with all the souls up and about and able to greet him, ease his transition." Fanny felt she might even look like Carrie. She was sitting ramrod straight, barely tipping her chin to sip her drink, so as not to dislodge the fourteen pins that were holding her hair up.

After a short struggle for sense, TX said, "Ah! Ghosts! Pumpkins! Hallo*ween*, I win." He looked at Fanny amused, with admiration. He admired her sitting there so grandly. He admired her trick, against all expectation, of making sense, although he had not eliminated the possibility that she was a space cadette, or a virgin, or something. It was because he couldn't make her out that he couldn't move along.

TX got Fanny laughing instead of crying about Candace, about the latest Amnesty International report, about their being slaughtered on Tuesday, Election Day, about the terrible lungs of Eskimos. "I mean we uncovered one of the most outrageous miscarriages of moral judgment. I fool you not. This is strictly straight. Do you know that it has now been discovered that the bad lungs of Eskimos, previously and confidently attributed to smoking and alcohol, are after all the consequence of breathing excessively cold air?" It was really one way to handle a lot of dismal data, this laughing, the cosmic joke, and Fanny was glad to be wiping her eyes. She had at first looked at TX with a little sinking of the heart, disconcerted by her own unheightened excitement at being once again with this extremely attractive man that she had reconstructed for herself while in France. There was some discrepancy.

They were stuffed with Peking Duck and he said, "Listen, something's come up. I think next week I'm going to be a mile high."

"You going to Denver?"

"Correct. You know Seminars at Corporate Encounters? Well, I'm moving over, and the thinking is (that's what we call it—thinking) that we get this package together. We set up a week of cultural enrichment for second-level executives and their wives in Vail, Colorado. It's going to be scholarly seminars, very serious. Nothing shallow. Reading lists, everything. In June when the academics get sprung. We want the real thing, no shit. Now I've been put in charge of selling the corporations, lining up the chalets, all that's in the works—but we need a *scholar* to coordinate the *content*. And immediately, of course, I thought of *you*." They both howled, but TX was nonetheless perfectly serious.

"It's free-lance, $400 a week," he said. Almost twice *First*.

Of course it was the sort of solid offer that begins to dissolve as soon as the words hit the open air. The clearance was held up until the first of the year—actually *after* the first of the year, and there was uncertainty about new tax-law and corporate write-offs with a new administration, but TX himself wasn't uncertain, and was able personally practically to assure Fanny that the job was hers. He was one of those cavalier optimists who guarantee that whatever you're worried about will turn out fine, and sometimes proves to be quite right. In this case he would so prove.

In the meanwhile Fanny became immediately engaged by the challenge of such a project, and on the spot began thinking of themes that would tie the courses together, "*Danes* in English literature, beginning with Beowulf, and Hamlet . . ."

"That's too gloomy. You got to find something upbeat."

"What about girls masquerading as boys, as for instance in *Twelfth Night* and Beethoven uses it in *Fidelio*, and let's see . . ."

"These are *second*-level, honey. They can't take anything kinky."

TX was flippant, but nonetheless severe in his expectations of the highest-quality cultural package, and Fanny was infected by his seriousness, her first example of sincere public relations—so infected, indeed, that she became alarmed at her own unworthiness to be the representative of the learned world. It infused her with purpose and a sense of mission. It had her writing letters for suggestions to Carrie, to Titus, and even to Junie Waterman. It sent her on a binge of self-improvement: terrifically serious reading (beginning with the first volume of Herzen's *My Life and Thoughts*); tracking through the city's smaller museums (getting quite friendly with a guard in the Morgan Library); attending free concerts, and as Christmas approached, facing a choice of twenty-eight *Messiahs*.

Witlessly she chose the wrong *Messiah*, in which Gina Reddish was playing in the orchestra, and afterwards they bumped into each other, and Gina said, "Hi! How are you? TX tells me he's thinking of taking you on. He's really quite impressed. He's very funny. He says he has to take a firm line with you. Otherwise you're liable to present the Moral Majority with a week of seminars on the History of Drag . . ."

"I didn't know you were in New York."

"Actually I'm not. I just take an engagement when I can get it, and TX puts me up. I'm lucky to have him."

"He's in Denver, isn't he?"

"He's coming back."

"Well, there are certainly a lot of *Messiahs*, I'm glad I chose this one," said Fanny lying.

"I think there are fourteen in Boston," said Gina.

Fanny found this remark infuriating.

"Well, I've got to run. Great to see you," she said.

The meeting with Gina put a crimp in Fanny's Christmas spirit. It laid out the undisguised and charmless facts, like things one brings home from a discount store, not wrapped up and tied with ribbon by a long shot. TX was a man of many attributes, and Fanny was interested to fall in love with him, and this love eluded her. He was not unethical, not dumb, he was certainly entertaining, and she liked to dress up and be seen with him, but she remained an observer of an act that was not really convincing—ultimately too dismissible. She wanted him to notice that he was lacking in substance—and mind that he was. But he was as amused by her preoccupations as she was distracted by his. He called her a berry gatherer. She certainly had reason to believe she was wandering around the wrong culture, a culture of spear hurlers—and not adapting.

"You know one thing I like about you?" she said to him. "You're not into disillusionment. You're immune." And she sent him a postcard which said, " 'Disillusionment is a vulgar, hackneyed word, a veil under which lie hidden the sloth of the heart, egoism posing as love, the noisy emptiness of vanity with pretensions to everything and strength for nothing.'—Alexander Herzen." It was the sort of message from Fanny that could have been written in Urdu. He didn't come from Urduland, as he said to himself, 96 percent without regret.

This asset of TX's, this undisillusionability, was not proving enough, could not carry the weight of Fanny's whole future, but the whiff of carefree Gina under her nose was once more a red herring. She was off on the chase again.

Carrie and Fanny were engaged in a marathon of letter writing, Fanny sending hers hot with the heat of immediacy of her feelings, reading prompt, thoughtful replies fourteen to sixteen days later. When, in January, Fanny wrote, "If this job does come through it will mean my going to Denver with TX," she was reading a response to a letter she had written in the throes of Gina-inspired gloom ("I don't know, any more, what ordinary hopes for life are . . .") to which Carrie was answering with a remark of Nadezhda Mandelstam: "To think that we could have had an ordinary family life with its bickering, broken hearts, and divorce suits! There are people in the world so crazy as not to realize that this is normal human existence of the kind everybody should aim at. What wouldn't we have given for such ordinary heartbreaks!" Further down in the letter, referring to Fanny's Cultural Themes, she wrote, "Titus thinks that you might choose a year like 1200 and then take, say, five soundings, depending on how many lectures are in your schedule—Paris (scholasticism), the English barons, Toulouse and the Cathar heresy, and so on . . ." Titus didn't write. Junie Waterman sent a postcard which said, enigmatically, "A serious writer needs a serious reader. J. W." Or egocentrically. Fanny had written two very long letters to Titus.

Finally, Fanny got the word. Her job would begin on the first of March. In the middle of February Carrie wrote, "I had wanted to come home for a visit, at least, after all these years, but I don't like to leave Lu. She's not quite right. Titus flew to Boston last Tuesday for two weeks. He has a friend who's been made headmaster of an old experimental school on Cape Ann. He's determined to bracket five years in order to teach adolescents history, see how much can really be done. He has a fierce sense of service."

Fanny made the calculation that Titus would have been in the States for two weeks. She stood in front of the kitchen calendar in a trance, figuring the days.

"What's the matter?" asked Missy.

"I was thinking I ought to go up to Boston to say good-bye before I leave."

"When?"

"Now."

"You mean tonight? It's seven o'clock!"

"I'll miss MacNeil-Lehrer."

Twenty-One

THE ground floor of the thread mill had been gutted, its
machinery sold at auction. It was now an empty oblong
lined with multipaned windows for nineteenth-century
workers to see by, but what could be seen in the dead of
winter even at high noon was a question. Twentieth-cen-
tury workers can't see by it. Titus was standing on a bench
at the far end of the factory floor, holding a flashlight to the
top of an architect's drawing nailed to the wall. There was
a section he hadn't been able to make out on his previous
inspections, scouting for Carrie. He thought it was as cold
as a cathedral or a mead hall. He clicked off his light,
turned to lean carefully against the wall plan, and, squinting into the void, decided it was three times the size of a
mead hall. The sun suddenly came out, casting a deep
skewed grid down the length of the damaged floor, and
moments later as abruptly disappeared, in the rhythm of
some immense stranded sea creature taking irregular
breaths—in a terminal state. Titus, suffering, identified
himself with this state. "I have been more ravished myself
than anybody since the Trojan War," he said to himself,

borrowing the words of Lord Byron. Still leaning against the wall, he saw the door at the far corner open. Not Beowulf. Nobody in furs and skins. Fanny in boots.

Fanny did not expect to, and did not, see Titus standing on a chair in the shadow of the other end. She wandered a few feet inside and stopped. The sun came out and the grid branded her painlessly. Five minutes might have passed while she stood thinking and listening. Titus, unable to move, watched. The boots, the skirt, her hair—she looked like Lara in *Dr. Zhivago*, a measure of his romantic love, or yet another example of the pervasive influence of the motion-picture industry in the twentieth century.

Finally, she called out a quick question: "Titus?"

"What?" he answered sharply, startled, and jumped off the bench.

"For *God's* sake! Titus!" she said, startled as well.

The "Tti-titus, what-what, God's sa-sake Ti" wavered through the emptiness and bounced against the walls. Also their laughing. They ambled towards each other, meeting in the middle, shaking hands, instead of the more impersonal hugging and kissing.

"What were you doing?" she asked him sternly, the tension still in her voice from the fright he gave her, and from watching herself turn her life right-side-up in sixteen hours.

"I was measuring the dimensions of a mead hall," he said. And instead of explaining, and instead of expressing relief, astonishment, joy, or even polite interest in Fanny's materialization, he said, "Come on. I'll show you the sketches Will's had drawn up for Carrie." And he threw himself into a long explication of the drawings. It was marvelously steadying.

Fanny hardly heard. She felt as though she were in a medley race and had finished one stroke and was resting, getting geared for the next. Off the top of her head she murmured a maundering refrain ("I don't see how Carrie can go through with this." "How can she leave Albi? Abandon everybody . . . sell the Printing House . . ." "Why would somebody like Junie settle for Boston?")

Titus was rattling off estimates of solar feasibility, interest rates, all the costs: "She's fussy," he said. "She doesn't want a Mead Hall Hilton. But it's not supposed to be another Printing House. It's not going to serve the same purpose. It's going to be a pension for Europeans—people the universities *strand* here—as they think. Actually Junie will love it. But as far as I can make out she's got to come up with another million bucks and I *know* she hasn't got collateral for money like that. Still, she's going ahead." He was standing, momentarily absorbed, his hands in his trouser pockets, looking for the other million on the factory floor. "There's got to be a silent partner. She was in love once upon a time, I guess she told you. Maybe he's the one with the big bucks . . ." He sounded dubious, however. He picked up the bench and carted it off to a sunny parallelogram, and would have moved more furniture if there had been any. They now sat down and got solar energy through their backs. It was very effective.

"She never mentioned *who* it was," Fanny said nervously, since it was Titus's father who had the big bucks and not Mr. Costello.

"I've always assumed it was an inside job, somebody on B Street—I'm ready to settle for Hugh Reddish," said Titus, not interested in pursuing Carrie's love.

Fanny looked mildly surprised at the offer of another susceptible father in a neighborhood so long characterized in her mind by its unusual familial integrity, but she was also not interested in pursuing Carrie's love. "My mother and I

came over for a visit and Lucia thought you might be here,"
said Fanny, who had had trouble shaking her mother.
"Lucia says you've made up your mind to join that pilot
school."

Lucia had been the conduit through which news from
Gina Reddish of Fanny's infatuation for this TX had
reached Titus. He felt the usual fondness for the bearer of
bad tidings. Made gloomy by the thought of Gina he said
gloomily, "It's a pilot school all right. Jefferson thought
every citizen should have three years of schooling so that he
would know how to read and write and protect his liberties.
They hope to accomplish the same thing in twelve years."

"It'll be a real breakthrough."

"They're on a shoestring, and it's even worse now on
account of the tax revolt. That means *no* studies on the
Early Film, of course not only as a matter of policy, but
also they haven't any audio-visual equipment, if you don't
count a stereopticon they found in the basement. Actually,
they're anxious to cultivate a negative attitude. *No!* is their
rallying cry. No study hall, no vandalism, no drugs, no
cars, no Second Chance, that sort of thing. There's even a
dress code. No jeans, some sort of collar, leather shoes. Even
the *teachers* have to obey the dress code."

"Carrie's influence must have run wild."

"It's a school that's considered very far-out, very fringe-y.
It may sound like strictly Bible Belt back-to-basics to
you, and if you were to teach there, it would be straight
Henry IV, Part I, I assure you. No new criticism, no semiotics, no deconstructon . . . Still, they've got the idea it's a
revolution. And they expect the world to beat a path to
their door.

"It must take a fantastic amount of *courage* to say *no jeans,*
no *semiotics,* and *mean* it."

" 'One will never know what acts of cowardice the fear of not appearing to be sufficiently to the left will have prompted our Frenchmen to commit.' Do you know who said that? Charles Péguy. Do you know who he was?"

"No! *Listen*, Titus, I really *wanted* to *see* you. I wrote you *two* letters and I never got an answer."

Titus sat bent over, his forearms resting on his knees, and he locked his fingers to make a church and a steeple. Fanny was sitting straight up in her new fashion, and when he didn't answer she felt entitled to press her claim: "Listen, I was really anxious to get some help from you for this new job. As soon as the possibility came up I found I hardly had to scrap around at all, looking for ideas. So many things you talked about just *rushed* into my head—I had more than enough themes, I had to *eliminate* several— 'Mutilating Protestants,' might make them nervous about their identity and they wouldn't sign up. You can't imagine how tactful you have to be to get a thing like this together, but I thought the history of *printing* would be both safe and instructive—and I'm reading Herzen, but I don't see what you can do with *that* in a week . . . but I also wrote you because I needed to know more about the use of land and Braudel's *longue durée* . . ." She paused. Titus said nothing. "I *asked* you," she continued quite heated, "because you *can't expect* those people to read Bloch or Braudel. *I* haven't read them. I never even *heard* of them. But I was altogether determined to use the ideas that interest you."

Titus tipped his head and looked at her with a crooked smile. "You mean as a favor?"

She was taken aback. The sun had caught his hair and made it golden for a moment. He has blond hair and blue eyes, she marveled to herself, a really misleading description. She got up in agitation and walked a circle of steps, and then, taking her stand a few feet beyond Titus's shadow, she dipped her brow against the sun and again addressed herself to his bent head: "Those days with you were the best in my life. I know I *learned* more *then* . . . I think of them a lot. They were playing Bach, Telemann, and *Piaf* on NPR all last *week*. It's Telemann's birthday. He's 300 years *old*. Piaf's really a cut above Judy Garland but you can't sing along . . ." She stopped again, not knowing where to go. She had gotten herself quite frantic. She was looking at him through actual tears. Finally she said in a rather hoarse voice, "*Titus*, why didn't you at least congratulate me on getting the *job?*"

Titus lifted his head and said quietly, with a mild smile, "The job? It really irritated the blooming shit out of me."

There was a long moment of assimilation while they looked soberly at each other, but then Fanny thought she'd never heard anything funnier, more heartening, and she said, grinning, "Is that so?"

"What the sweet hell do you think you're doing? Do you think you can remain unaffected—personally *uncompromised*—while committing yourself to the new and trendy profession of trivializing learning? You say you're obsessed by the need to live a worthwhile life, and some fancy PR guy comes along and snaps his fingers and you're cured! You say you don't want to be carried about by every wind, but when an offer turns up with absolutely no ballast whatsoever, you sail off like a goddamn Tinkerbell. It's not as if you had no choice. After all, you aren't one of the oppressed people, you aren't one of the *superfluous* people— now you're into Herzen. It's not escargots and white wine or the gutter. *You* can *choose* . . ."

Fanny stood at the end of his shadow, clutching her arms

against the cold, calmed, with only a buzzing in her head. She said, "I did choose."

"A couple of years," he went on, now full-steam, "and you'll say you're caught up in it, you'll think of yourself as a *helpless victim* of a corrupt society. I really hate fake victims . . . Oh well, it's all very trite, Fanny . . . and of course you might find it insufferable that I say things like this . . . but I'm impelled to say them for a reason even triter. I've fallen in love with you."

Fanny closed her eyes, took a deep breath, opened her eyes, and said with one-half of a smile, "And you want me to give up trying to make it, now that I've finally got my foot on the first rung? Exchange the opportunity to bring intellectual enrichment to corporate America? in luxury chalets? nestled in the soaring Rockies?—for the chance to lure children with medieval history and Shakespeare from sex and violence in *Rockport?*

"Marblehead."

"It's an offer difficult to resist."

"Once in a lifetime."

Fanny still stood tall, unmoving, her mind shuffling. Titus still sat, his arms leaning on his knees. After a few moments Fanny said, "I'm apt to take you literally. And I think I would need to have some public avowal . . . a bumper sticker: Fanny Foote Ah Luv Yew, or a marriage license. Because the bobbing, the drifting, the episodic— that's what I don't want. Junie talks about its being the age of the short story. I don't want to live a lot of short stories . . . But I think I'm terribly in love with you."

Fanny gave a little lurch and in a moment they were finally in each other's arms.

Some time passed. They then resumed sitting on the

bench, holding hands in an archaic manner, and in what was definitely a mead hall. Otherwise they would have been able to tear themselves away—if it had been only a dank and gutted factory.

"Lucia says you fly back to Paris tonight."

"I've finally got it arranged to work three months at l'École des Hautes Études. Jesus, I was really anxious to get it. Now I can't remember why. But I think I can wrap everything up and be back by the Fourth of July. Would you like to be married on the Fourth of July? What do you think? Do you suppose we could get married first, and *then* make love?"

It was unorthodox but they meant to go through with it anyway.